THE
GAME
OF
WAR

RENE FOMBY

Book Ness
Monster
Press

Book Ness
Monster
Press

Book Ness Monster Press 4530 Blue Ridge Drive
Belton, Texas 76513

Copyright © 2017 by Rene Fomby.

Paperback ISBN: 9781947304017

Visit us on the World Wide Web: http://www.renefomby.com

Fomby, Rene. The Game of War. Book Ness Monster Press.
Paperback Edition.

To Elizabeth.

foreword

Much of this book is the product of some three decades or so that I spent in the world of personal computing and video gaming, starting with an all-too short stint in marketing at Xerox Office Systems, the group that invented most of what makes up modern computing. The group that then gave it all away to focus its full its full attention on selling copiers. Look how well that worked out.

After Xerox, my career bounced between various aspects of the pharmaceutical and computer industries, and sometimes at the nexus of both. In the process I had the wonderful opportunity to meet and work with some of the giants of personal computing, and many of the stories sprinkled throughout this book reflect the many days and nights I spent in Redmond and Cupertino. Several movies and television shows have attempted to capture the craziness and magic of the early years of the Macintosh and PCs, but none of them really do it justice. You kinda had to be there.

Finally, while I have tried to make this book as realistic as possible, certain aspects of the story seem all too real, all too prescient of future events. I can only hope that this piece of fiction stays just that.

the rocket ship

1

Sanders crouched low along the back row of seats in the crowded Situation Room, trying to keep a wary eye on the President while still managing to stay out of eyesight himself. Up front, the Director of Naval Intelligence was wrapping up an assessment of the recent build-up of the Chinese fleet. DNI had a laser pointer highlighting highly enlarged photos of two new aircraft carriers the Chinese had just launched from its shipyards in Dalian, years ahead of Naval Intelligence's best-case projections.

The next slide showed keels being laid in Dalian for two more flattops. Although the Chinese navy was still too small to pose any real threat to the United States, he understatedly explained that the speed at which they were launching new warships was... disconcerting. DNI switched to an overview of the South China Sea, zooming in on the Spratley Islands, a disputed archipelago of fourteen islands and more than 100 coral reefs lying off the coasts of Malaysia, the Philippines and southern Vietnam. The Chinese had already transformed more than a dozen of these reefs into virtual aircraft carriers, dumping sand and other material onto the reefs using hundreds of dredges and barges, including a giant self-propelled dredger, the Tian Jing Hao. China's strategic objective in building the "Great Wall of Sand" was to challenge American naval supremacy in the Far East. And that made America's Southeast Asia Treaty Organization allies very nervous.

DNI ceded the floor to presentations from several other directorates, each of them equally alarming. American leadership was being challenged around the globe, with Russia and China becoming increasingly belligerent and nationalistic as their economies stalled. The Western response to this threat was being hamstrung by Europe's unwillingness to step up to the plate in regards to their commitments to NATO. As a result, the United States continued to bear an ever increasing share of the cost of NATO, while at the same time the Europeans consistently tried to avoid any direct confrontation with the suddenly aggressive Russian army. Meanwhile, back in the States, Congress seemed dead set on opposing any modernization strategies drawn up by military planners, clinging instead to patchwork extensions of outdated weapons systems in an attempt to protect key factory jobs and votes back in their home districts.

It was clear to Sanders that this trend couldn't be allowed to continue without dire and possibly irreversible consequences to America's national security. The new President appeared to be cautiously responsive to his advisors' warnings, but Sanders knew that support voiced in the quiet confidences of the Situation Room could be quite different from what emerged in the heat of political battle.

Still, Operation Beekeeper remained a go, and any material change in that status would come at a very heavy cost. Sanders silently prayed that this President understood exactly how much was at stake in the end. *Lord, please give this president the strength to see this through. And give us the wisdom to make it work.*

And to that end, he had a plane to catch.

2

The room was hot and close, with too many bodies packed in far too tight in front of the sixty-inch flat screen monitor. Someone had thought to pull the drapes loosely across the lone window to shut out the light, but through a slight crack Marc thought he could just see the top of the Eiffel Tower across the street.

Boston and Bay Area had just finished up. That left New York, and then, finally, Austin. Him. Marc glanced around, checking out the crowd. No one in the room seemed very impressed so far, and frankly, neither was he. The two previous presentations just hadn't broken any new ground. They had both seemed uninspired, derivative. Been there, done that. Not that he could have done any better. Way in the back of the crowd, in a darkened corner, Marc noticed one person that didn't seem to fit into this nerdy gathering. Tall, with close-cropped hair, a square jaw and a stiff posture, he was busily scribbling into a small notebook. And not a real notebook. The paper kind, with a wire binding. Odd.

New York was up next. A girl and a guy. That was certainly something you didn't see every day. He couldn't quite place their ages. Somewhere between seventeen and twenty five. The sweet spot. Marc suddenly felt very old.

Up front, a short, bald-headed guy who was apparently running the show nodded his head. The lights dropped, and New York launched into their presentation. Marc felt his stomach

4

dropping, like he was on a roller coaster and had just finished the slow, agonizing crawl to the top. If realism was the sole criterion for judging this contest — and Marc knew it was very high on the list — these guys had already won. In a race that had no prizes for place and show.

Then it was over. Several people in the audience began to clap, and Marc's stomach dropped a little further. Baldy looked over at him, a hungry smile playing across his face. It was his turn. Marc was starting to sweat, not the least because he had no idea how his demo was going to turn out. Dave had uploaded some last-minute changes to him while he was still in the air. And while they had assumed they could run the demo on their own gamer laptop, it turns out they should have thought to dive a little deeper into the rules. Rules that said the contest would take place on a lower-end server, so none of the contestants had a hardware advantage.

New York girl stood up and he walked over to take her seat, a keyboard, mouse and gamepad laid out in front of him. With a few quick keystrokes he loaded the software. Everything was ready. Baldy nodded again, the lights dimmed, and the big show began. In the city of shows. Las Vegas.

Marc clicked the mouse button. He and Dave were now all in on the biggest gamble of their lives.

3

The billboard outside the airport trumpeted the city's signature slogan: What Happens in Vegas Stays in Vegas. *God, I hope not.* Marc leaned back, stretching to find an extra inch of leg room, his 6'4" frame stuffed into the middle seat on the Southwest Airlines CES Special back into Austin.

The demo at the Bellagio had gone well, even with all of the embarrassing software glitches. *Heck, even Bill Gates got slammed by the Blue Screen of Death a time or two.* Marc took another sip from his beer as he tapped out some next steps on his tablet. The boys from Redmond — or wherever they were from — seemed to like what they saw, even offering a hint that a next generation Xbox console was looming that might solve some of the sluggish multithreading issues. Issues they hadn't caught on their gaming laptop, but had been mortifyingly unmistakable on the slower demo server in the hotel room.

He thought about Dave, about what he needed to share with his partner about the contest, then turned his focus back to the tablet. *What is the timing — can we launch with new console?* he typed. Marc paused, then added a short list of the problems that had popped up during the ten minute demo.

He glanced down at his watch, his mind already slipping into code mode. The plane would touch down in less than an hour. He'd ask Dave to grab a pizza to go from Mangia's, and they could dig into the source of the ghosting and the crashes while the memory of what had caused all the problems was still fresh. Elle would just have to understand. Again.

4

His ride was already waiting at the curb. Marc tossed his carry on across the back seat and jumped in. Checking his phone, he saw that he had an email waiting from Dovetail, suggesting a meeting later in the week. Paul Jackson and Tim Gatland were going to be in New York until Friday, which made the meeting a lot more convenient than flying out to Dovetail's headquarters in Chatham, Kent.

The plan was to build *Dronewars* on top of the Microsoft Flight Simulator engine, which Microsoft had licensed to Lockheed Martin and Dovetail Games after the company shut down Aces Studio and their in-house flight simulator development team in 2009. Although the PC-based Microsoft Flight Simulator X game was still on the market, and passionately supported by the online flight simulator community, the last Microsoft-based version had been released in 2006. That was well over a decade ago, and the game had still never made it to Xbox. Dovetail launched a Steam version in 2014 for the PC, while Lockheed was mainly focused on military and commercial applications of the technology.

The Xbox team had suggested they might be able to swing a licensing deal for the simulator code, but Marc knew that the real key to getting the game ported to Xbox meant finding the right coders, not rights to the code. The *Dronewars* demo was currently running on Windows 10, using Lockheed's developer version of the program. Fine for early concept development and testing, but the software needed to be ported to Xbox, and soon. Dovetail already had *Fishing* and *Train Simulator* running on Xbox, and had deep experience in running multiplayer gaming on top of Steamworks, so a partnership with them might make sense. But a partnership would also mean a loss of control.

Marc shot back an email suggesting a lunch meeting on Friday. He could fly out and back the same day. He checked the available flights, feeling a familiar clench in his gut as the prices popped up. Another dip into the startup fund, and yet another reminder that a Kickstarter campaign was well overdue. *The burn rate is starting to heat up.*

5

Dave was polishing off a slice of pepperoni and jalapeño pizza when Marc finally strolled in to the small North Lamar apartment they were using as a temporary office. Dave hooked a thumb toward the refrigerator. "Want a beer? Still have a six-pack of Torpedos in there."

Marc shook his head. "Nah. Too much going on tonight. And I already had a beer on the plane. I'm gonna have to stick to DP tonight." He grabbed a Dr Pepper Ten out of the refrigerator, threw a slice of pizza onto a paper plate and plopped down in front of the dual-screen development box. By using two monitors, it was easy to track and modify source code on one screen while testing out the changes on the other.

"How's Jules?" Marc asked as he reached over to tap the shift key, waking the PC up from sleep mode.

"About the same. Not happy," Dave answered. Dave and Julia had been dating for almost a year, so the relationship had straddled Dave's job at Google and his new venture with Marc. Rocketship.

An auburn Amazon with a killer body, Julia had first met Dave when he was still a Google Software God. Young, rich and arrogant. A black BMW M convertible, dinner at all the best Bay Area restaurants. Now Dave was driving a Honda, and dinner was more likely at El Patio or Mama Fu's.

"I had planned to take her out to dinner at Justine's tonight, to celebrate the demo. After the last few weeks, she's been feeling pretty neglected. Can't say I really blame her." Nailing the demo at the Consumer Electronics Show had been a real coup, and Dave and Marc had burned the candles and quite a few cases of Diet Coke adding last-minute features to the game as fast as they could in the three short weeks they had available. They took Christmas Eve and Christmas Day off, and Marc convinced Dave that there would have been an open insurrection if they reneged on taking Julia and Elle to the Bob Schneider show at the Paramount on New Year's Eve, particularly since they had already blown several hundred dollars apiece for the tickets. Still, the girls made it clear they weren't at all enthusiastic about constantly taking a backseat to Dave and Marc's new mistress, *Dronewars.*

Dave and Marc both suspected that Julia would be the first casualty of the new venture. She deeply resented Dave's decision to quit Google and partner with Marc in a gaming startup. And Julia wasn't shy about sharing that opinion. Dave knew Julia could have just about any man she wanted, and the man she wanted — the Google version of Dave Elliott, with dark shaggy hair and steel-blue eyes, a man who partied almost as hard as he worked — simply no longer existed. The new Dave drove a *Honda*, for God's sake. It was just a matter of time before she gave up on him entirely and moved back to California.

Elle was a different story. After earning a BS in computer science at Stanford, she went to work at Amgen, where she led a complete overhaul of their social media strategy and tracking. She met Marc, then a rising young product manager at Google, during a routine training session on social media analytics at Googleplex, Google's Mountain View headquarters. Elle had joined several Google team members for lunch at Root, one of around thirty cafés on the Googleplex campus. She had just finished her meal and was grabbing an iced coffee to go at the coffee bar when, turning around too quickly, she lost her grip on the coffee, and in a second Marc was wearing the entire cup. In her embarrassment, Elle offered to make it up to him by buying him dinner that evening. Four months later she moved into his apartment, and when Google sent Marc to Austin, Elle quit her job at Amgen and moved to Austin with him.

Thanks to a 790 on the GMAT and a 3.8 undergrad GPA, Elle applied for and was immediately accepted into the MBA program at the University of Texas, concentrating in marketing and entrepreneurship. She was now only a semester into the program, but already the core classes on accounting and time value of money were having an indelible impact on her. And on her plans for becoming a key contributor to Rocketship.

All of that was the last thing on Marc's mind as he pulled up the source code for the game on the left screen and the demo on the right. "I had a chance to run through the code in the Vegas airport, and I think the ghosting is coming from this section, where we manage sprite generation. Somehow I think the multithreading is getting out of sync, creating problems in managing the resource arrays. That could also explain why we're leaking resources during the action sequences."

Dave pulled up a chair and squinted at the code Marc had highlighted. "Does it really matter, Marc? I mean, all this code is ultimately just going to be scrapped once we go MMO."

"Yeah, well, MMO is still a ways off, and meanwhile we need to be able to test all the new features without it always crashing on us. Plus, *you* didn't have to demo the damn thing today. It looks really bad if we can't keep it lit for longer than two minutes at a time in full fight mode. I have to show this to Dovetail, maybe as early as this Friday, and I need them fully convinced that we have the technical huevos to pull this off."

"You mean *I* have the technical huevos, Mr. Jobs," Dave jabbed, suggesting that his partner was, as they say in Texas, all hat and no cattle.

Marc grinned back. "Well, excuse me, Mr. Wozniac, but this shit don't sell itself. Someone has to be the showman in this company. Just be glad I don't make you run it on an all-white Xbox with a single button joystick!"

6

Massively Multiplayer Online Gaming, or MMO, is a form of computer-based video gaming that allows large numbers of gamers to play against or with each other simultaneously over a network, usually using some form of virtual reality.

The very first MMO was developed at Xerox PARC in Palo Alto, where the scientists and engineers who created the original What You See Is What You Get (WYSIWYG) computers and Ethernet local area networking built a rudimentary galactic conquest game in the early 1980's. Dozens of Xerox researchers simultaneously blasted away at each another in virtual rocket ships, working feverishly to annihilate the other side. In 1986, a company called Kesmai released a 2D flight combat simulation game called Air Warrior on the GEnie online service. And the most successful MMO of all was World of Warcraft, boasting almost 9 million subscribers at its peak.

The biggest technical hurdle for MMO games is the challenge of synchronizing the game action across a large number of simultaneous users. For some games this problem can be pretty minimal. But for combat style games involving fast and furious movement, delays in the game action destroy the illusion of realism. And even more critical, when a player shoots an opponent at point-blank range he expects that opponent to be hit, not missed because the opposing player's avatar moved but the shooter's screen hadn't quite caught up to the changes.

To solve this problem, game play in modern combat-type MMOs is coordinated by high-powered dedicated servers, with each server capable of handling up to five thousand active players. These servers continuously update not only the position of each player, but also factors like direction, speed, shooting status and accumulated damage. More importantly, the servers manage time synchronization across all of the online players, which is critical to the games' physics simulations as well as scoring and damage detection.

In the specialized area of multiplayer flight simulators, a group called VATSIM —Virtual Air Traffic Simulation Network — operates a dedicated worldwide Internet-based flight-simulation network with over 200,000 members. VATSIM lets users of flight simulation software such as Microsoft Flight Simulator or Lockheed's Prepar3D simulate real-time communications with virtual air traffic controllers, and has proven to be a powerful tool for training new pilots in critical communications skills without bogging down real ATC communications channels or, worse, risking dangerous communications errors that could cause air traffic conflicts and accidents.

A 2014 study showed there were an estimated 23.4 million active MMO subscribers worldwide. Global revenue generated by MMO games totals around fifteen billion U.S. dollars annually, with 2.5 billion dollars of that coming from North America alone. In other words, there was easy money to be made for anyone who could come up with a compelling new MMO game. And Marc and Dave were betting most of their life savings that *Dronewars* would be just that.

7

Dave had missed the CES demo because he had to fix a major bug in the *Dronewars* software and couldn't get it debugged before the flight to Vegas. Their tickets were on Southwest, so he was able to get credit for the missed flight to use later. But the ticket to New York to meet with Dovetail was going to be booked on United, so the $1,200 cost of the round-trip ticket was completely out-of-pocket. Despite the added cost, though, Marc agreed that Dave needed to join him for the Dovetail meeting. Dave was the company's Paul Allen, after all, and missing the meeting would make them seem desperate and underfunded. Which, as a matter of fact, they were.

Something had come up at Dovetail at the last minute and neither Jackson nor Gatland could make the meeting, but they sent two underlings in their place: Hal Porter, their marketing director for flight sim, and Bob Tandy, an Xbox developer. Marc and Dave met the Dovetail duo at The Smith restaurant in Midtown New York. The Smith was a popular American Brasserie, famous among New Yorkers for using fresh local produce. The restaurant was crowded and very noisy, but the wait for a table near the bar was mercifully short. The four men quickly placed their orders, and as the waiter delivered their drinks, just as quickly got down to business.

Porter leaned across the table. "Look, let's put our cards on the table. I had a chance to check in with some of my contacts in Redmond, and they told me about the demo, and what you're trying

17

to pull off. I don't really want to eyeball any of your software, and frankly, doing so might be a bit of a problem down the road." He settled back, his eyes dancing between Marc and Dave. "Here's the net of it. Dovetail is a well-established gaming company, with rock-solid credentials in MMO, flight sim, and now Xbox. You, on the other hand, are a dirt-poor startup with little more than a dream and a dot-com site. You and a million other dreamers, all in the same leaky boat. With your software and five bucks, I could almost buy a cup of coffee at Starbucks. So I'm not seeing where you bring anything to the table that Dovetail would want." Porter sat back, sharing a smile that didn't quite make it all the way up to his eyes.

For perhaps the first time in years, Marc seemed at a loss for words. Nothing in the various emails that had passed between him and Dovetail had prepared him for this kind of blow-off. He quickly checked Dave's reaction to all this, and noted his friend's growing look of concern. Marc swallowed hard and turned back to Porter. In for a penny, in for a pound. "First of all, Hal, we're not just your average startup." He hoped the use of Porter's first name might help soften the tone between them. "Before we started this company, Dave here was one of Google's top software engineers. The best of the best. And as for me, I won the top award in marketing for my division two years out of the last five. So, net-net, we know what we're doing, and by any metric we're pretty much the best in the damn universe at doing it."

Now it was Marc's turn to sit back a bit, showing a confidence he didn't actually feel. "Second, the fact is, we don't need

18

you." He caught a brief flash of panic in Dave's eyes beside him, but pushed on. "The core flight sim software is damn near open source. Lockheed will sublicense it to us for a song, and our mutual friends at Microsoft have already indicated they're willing to sell us a license as well. Xbox developers are a dime a dozen. MMO technology is old school, so no real secrets there. So it's not like you're the only gal at the dance. Just one of many. And that means what's really on the table here is whether you're interested in dancing with a good partner, or just want to sit by yourself in the corner while everyone else has all the fun."

During Marc's speech, Porter's face gradually shifted from insolent to angry. Now Marc could see Porter's neck beginning to turn red, and realized he had probably overplayed his hand. "Tell you what, *boy wonder*." Porter's eyes had taken on a dangerous glare. "You go ahead and shock the world with your amazing new game. Port it over to Xbox with your dime-a-dozen unemployed programmers, about all you can afford on your puny savings and the nickels and pennies you can find in your couch. And when you do go under, maybe, *maybe* I'll notice and throw the bankruptcy court a few thousand for the rights to your code. Dollars, not pounds sterling. In the meantime, this meeting is OVER!"

Porter stood up and stalked out. Tandy, unsure of what had just transpired, mumbled a quick apology and strode after him. Just then, the waiter arrived with the four lunches. Marc started to stand, thought better of it. "Check, please," he told the waiter, then stole a

19

quick look at Dave, who looked every bit like he had just swallowed a turd.

8

For Dave, the trip back to LaGuardia was pretty much a blur. Porter's insults kept ringing in his ears. It wasn't so much that Porter's comments were insulting — the bad part was that they rang so *true*.

Dave had been a superstar at Google, a superstar in a universe of fellow superstars. After graduating from Cal Tech at twenty, Dave became a lead programmer and designer for Google Lively, working directly under engineering manager Niniane Wang. Lively was an avatar-based virtual chatroom, where cartoon-like characters talked to each other using pop-up cartoon bubbles. Intended as a simpler, easier-to-use version of Second Life, Lively's simplicity ultimately became its downfall — the boredom factor set in very quickly, and Lively was shut down in December 2008, just six months after its debut.

Dave moved on to similar projects, ultimately working on Google Glass, eyeglasses that overlaid virtual reality on top of actual reality, and then as a key developer of Google Earth Flight Simulator, an add-on to Google Earth that let you fly a virtual airplane through the Google Earth landscape.

It was while Dave was working on GEFS that he was first approached by Marc Cullen. Marc was a concept guy who had built a reputation at Google for designing break-through approaches to user interface design and for enhancing the functionality of existing apps. He was also very personable, and much of his success at

Google could probably be traced to the fact that he was just, well, likeable. A natural salesman.

Dave had finished up his typical ten hour work day at Google and was just polishing off a flight of beers at JP Das. Most of the after work crowd had begun to filter out — some heading home, some heading out, a few heading back to work. Marc had already downed two growlers of ale, and it showed. He was holding court, as usual, but that court was quickly draining down to just the two of them.

"Dave, you just gotta look at the big picture." Marc downed the last of his ale and motioned across the room to a waitress, signaling for one more. "I mean, Google is great and all, but how long have you been working here, and where are you going?" Marc paused, swirling his empty growler. "Let's face it, we're both almost thirty, and what do we have to show for it? Money, great cars, even better girlfriends. But is that all there is? Just another replaceable pawn in the great Google game of chess? Hey, pick up your phone and google 'wiki Dave Elliott'. What do you get? Nothing! Same for me. Might as well be the invisible man. There's just gotta to be more to life that that. To our futures."

"I don't know, Marc." Dave contemplated the last sip of his beer. "Money, cars and Julia — that's pretty much my dream. And the projects I get to work on at Google, the people I get to work with, that's pretty much any nerd's wet dream. It's like getting paid to play, like being a pro quarterback without all the hitting and the injuries." Dave's head was a little woozy, and he decided he'd had enough. Any more and Julia wasn't going to be very happy with him when he stumbled home.

"That's just it, Dave. Name the worst starting quarterback for the worst team in football. How about the Browns? Over the last few years, they've fielded a new starting QB every few months, but you can name every single one of them. They're *stars*, Dave! Manziel, Weeden, Ogden, they all have wiki pages. And money that makes us look like paupers." Marc's third growler arrived, and he went silent for a moment while the waitress cleared the table. "I'm just sayin', you and me, we could do better. We've got talent, ideas, a shitload of money in the bank. We don't need Google, Dave, Google needs *us*. Google *uses* us. Maybe it's time we used ourselves for a change."

Dave knew it was just the beer talking. He had watched a lot of people strike out on their own to create the 'next big thing', only to discover that creating a blockbuster app was a lot easier on paper than it was in real life. With limited resources — never a problem at Google — deadlines would slip, seemingly unsolvable technical problems would pop up, money would drain away at an alarming rate. And, in the end, even if the app got finished and launched, the rest of the world usually refused to see the real vision, the brilliance. The dogs just wouldn't eat the dog food. At that point, broke — and broken — they would crawl back to Google, or Apple, or Microsoft, only to find out the door had been shut and locked behind them. The big tech giants wanted their superstars loyal, and with a seemingly endless supply of new talent begging to be let through the golden

23

gates, recycling talent that had proven to be disloyal was low on the list of recruiting priorities.

And so much of the success of new startups was just random. More a matter of being in the right place at the right time than any kind of meritocracy. Microsoft was probably the best example of this. As personal computers emerged onto the tech scene in the mid 1970's, Bill Gates and his childhood friend Paul Allen saw an opportunity to write a BASIC interpreter for the new MITS Altair 8800 computer. Lacking an actual Altair to develop and test their interpreter, Allen created a simulation of the new personal computer, running on a minicomputer at Harvard, where Gates was a student. They arranged to demo the software for MITS president Ed Roberts in Albuquerque in March, 1975. While on the plane to Albuquerque, however, Allen realized he had forgotten a key component of the software — a way to actually load the code onto the Altair computer! Frantically, he wrote a boot loader in machine language as the plane was on final descent. Amazingly, the program — and the boot loader — worked flawlessly, and Allen and Gates licensed the BASIC interpreter to MITS on the spot, forming a partnership they called 'Micro-soft'.

But first-year sales for the new company totaled only sixteen thousand dollars, with only three employees: Gates, Allen and Ric Weiland. The next year, the number grew to just over twenty-two thousand dollars and six employees. By 1980, the company, still almost entirely focused on programming languages, had annual revenues of a hair over $8,000,000 with only 40 employees.

That was when lady luck knocked on the door. IBM had decided to launch a personal computer of their own, based upon the new 16-bit Intel 8086 microprocessor. But the project had little support within IBM, and the IBM PC team was forced to cobble together a working computer using off-the-shelf components. The dominant personal computer operating system of the time was CP/M, short for Control Program for Microcomputers, a product of Gary Kildall's company, Digital Research. But CP/M only ran on old 8-bit computers, and IBM wanted Kildall to update the software to run on the new 16-bit Intel microprocessors. According to legend, when the IBM execs showed up at Digital Research's headquarters to discuss licensing CP/M-86 for their new computer, Kildall was a no-show — he was out at the airport trying out a new single engine airplane he had bought. He eventually showed up late to the meeting, but the die was cast. The IBM team flew up to Bellevue, Washington, to meet with Gates and Microsoft, whose programming language products were as dominant in their niche as CP/M was among operating systems.

Gates sold IBM on licensing his version of CP/M-86, asking only $50,000 for the rights but — importantly — reserving the right to sell a version of the operating system to makers of IBM PC-knockoff computers, commonly called clones. The only snag was, at the time of the meeting with IBM, Microsoft didn't actually *have* a CP/M type operating system. But Gates knew that Tim Paterson at Seattle Computer Products had written a CP/M derivative called 86-DOS to run on their own 8086-based computers. Keeping the IBM deal a secret, Gates arranged to license non-exclusive rights to the code from Paterson. (DOS stood for Disk Operating System, a reference to the fact that these computers were capable of storing programs and data on the exciting new 5 1/4 inch floppy disks). Microsoft polished up the operating system almost overnight, and IBM launched it as PC-DOS.

Microsoft received no revenue from the sales of PC-DOS, other than the initial licensing fee. But the launch of the IBM PC was quickly followed by the launch of "IBM compatible" clones from other companies, in particular transportable computers from Compaq that looked very much like sewing machines. These clones needed to run the same software as the IBM PC, including PC-DOS. But IBM had no interest in selling PC-DOS to its competitors, so into that void stepped Bill Gates and Microsoft with PC-DOS repackaged as MS-DOS , or Microsoft DOS. By year end 1982, company sales topped $24 million and headcount had soared to 220 employees. And that very same year Microsoft Flight Simulator for MS-DOS was launched.

With all of this in mind, Dave knew that the likelihood of becoming the next Bill Gates was next to zero, while the likelihood of crashing and burning was almost guaranteed. But the drunk across the table from him was on a roll, so Dave just sat back and let him talk.

"All we really need, Dave, is a killer idea, and we're golden. And the best ideas are always pretty simple. Take VisiCalc, for example. I know Dan Bricklin was a genius, but at its heart VisiCalc was just a regular expression parser with a UI wrapped around it. You could write that in a night, in your sleep."

Dave just shook his head. "Yeah, well, Bricklin was just mimicking some things electronically that had already been done on paper. And he had a good grasp of business, of what people in the business world needed. You and I are clueless about all that, pal. Plus, the days of being able to market bagware to businesses are long gone. The low hanging fruit has all been eaten."

Marc was undaunted. "Okay, so the oranges and bananas and apples are all gone. But what about the new fruit? What about goji berries? Stuff that's still on the edge, that the average person doesn't even know about yet?"

"You mean like phone apps? Put something out for the iPhone or Android to compete with the other four billion apps already in the stores? Hey, I have an idea, let's focus on smart watches. Make it a free app, but charge $3.99 for the 'professional' upgrade. We'll clean up!" Dave signaled the waitress to bring his check.

"Hey, don't give up on the idea so quickly, Dave. Let me think this over a bit. There's got to be an app space out there that we can fit into better than anyone else, something where we start off from day one with a big advantage. I mean, look at what we see day in and day out at Google. We have eyeballs on a literal fire hose of ideas. And real experience with turning those ideas into products. We just need to stop and pick one for ourselves, pick a goji berry that nobody else is focusing on. Just one good idea, and we'll take off like a rocket ship!" The waitress had returned with their checks. Marc handed over a credit card without checking the totals. "Don't worry, I got ya covered. We'll call it startup costs."

Dave mumbled his thanks, and when the waitress returned with the credit card slips, Marc quickly signed them, scribbling 'startup costs' across the top of the copy he stuffed in his back pocket.

That was the last Dave saw of Marc until two months later, when Marc texted him to meet for lunch at Charlie's Place, one of the free Google cafés on the main campus. Charlie's Place was named for Google's first lead chef, Charlie Ayers, who was also the head chef for the Grateful Dead before coming to Google.

When Dave arrived, he saw that Marc had already nabbed a table outside and was digging into a bowl of noodles. "Hey, Dave! Grab some grub and get over here." The noodles smelled good and were loaded with tons of shrimp and dungeness crab, so Dave headed for the seafood counter, grabbing a cold Topo Chico on his way back.

"What's hangin', Marc?" Dave had missed breakfast, so he tied into the noodles with gusto.

"Only good things, brother," Marc replied. "Well, good *ideas*, that is."

Dave raised an eyebrow quizzically. "What kind of ideas?"

Marc reached into a bag sitting beside him on the ground and pulled out several sheets of paper. Dave couldn't help but smile.

"Whoa, Marc, going old school on me? What is that — celluloid technology?"

Marc leaned forward, pushing the paper across the table. "Very funny. Sometimes writing on paper just seems more natural to me than typing or swyping on a tablet. Especially when I'm being creative. Like writing on a whiteboard during brainstorming sessions. Everything just seems to flow better."

Dave reached over and picked up the first page. "So what kind of brainstorming is this?" The top of the page was labeled "Core Strengths."

Marc pushed his noodles to the side and leaned closer. "Okay, so, back to the conversation we had a while back. The killer app. You remember how you suggested we needed to start with our core strengths, something where we had a natural edge on the competition?"

"I remember *you* suggesting that, but, okay, I'll go along with that idea. Where does that take us?" Dave's eyes were already halfway down the page.

"Well, I started by listing some areas where you and I have experience, the things we've been successful with at Google."

Dave saw the bullet points under his name. "And, for me at least, that would be Lively, Glass and Google Earth Flight Sim."

"Right. And what exactly do all of those have in common?"

"You mean, other than the fact that they're all online apps, and all by Google, driven off the Google databases? And the fact that the first two never really took off, and the last one is just a nice-to-have add-on to Google Earth, with no practical significance?"

Marc nodded his head. "Exactly. No practical use whatsoever. For any of them. But dive deeper than that. What is the common denominator?"

Rather than diving deeper, Dave mentally pulled back, trying to see the big picture in all of it. Something about each of them, some common thread. Then, like a fog lifting, he saw it. "Virtual reality."

"Yeah! That's it! Virtual reality! All three apps come down to plopping a virtual reality interface on top of actual reality. With Lively, you use an avatar as a representation of your physical self, sitting in a virtual chat room that seems for all intents and purposes like a real room. Google Glass involved, among other things, imposing layers of virtual information on top of what your eyes are actually seeing in the real world. And Earth Flight Sim let you fly a virtual plane as a metaphor for moving across the Google Earth landscape."

Dave was lost in thought. "Right, so in many ways that makes me an expert on building and interacting with virtual worlds. Or at least cartoon versions of virtual worlds. But where does that get us? A lot of companies have been dumping fortunes into the VR money pit, and not a single one of them has anything to show for it but proof of concept videos and apps."

"Not exactly. You are spot on if you're talking seamless VR, VR that makes you believe that you are actually interacting with a virtual world. And the biggest problem with that has always been the user interface, the challenge of how to manipulate the virtual world in a way that seems natural and intuitive to the user. But what if you took those two requirements away? What if you left the simulation more on the level of Lively, where the user is well aware of the limitations of the sim?"

"But that wouldn't be real VR. That would be more along the lines of a game, something like *Doom*, where you're just modeling a fake reality."

"Right. But *Doom* revolutionized the game industry, because even a fake reality is compelling if the action is right. Add in multiplayer, like all the Xbox games with four guys huddled in Mom's basement with old pizza boxes, pounding away at their controllers, or, on another level, MMO games, and the difference between reality and fake reality starts to fade completely away."

"So your killer app idea is to build another video game?"

"Not just another video game, Dave. The ultimate MMO. Massive multiplayer on a level that has never been tried before. Not thousands of players simultaneously, but tens of thousands. Maybe even hundreds of thousands."

"But that's impossible. You could never hope to time sync all those nodes in real time. Besides, who in the world would want to play a game like that? Anything and everything a player accomplished would be watered down by the sheer scale of the game. And how could you possibly cram all that many avatars onto a single battlefield?"

31

Dave was slowly catching up to where Marc had been for several weeks, sorting out the issues and digging for answers. "Okay, Dave, I don't have an answer for the time sync problem yet, but, hey, you can't work at Google and be put off by concerns about how to scale an application. As for the other issues, what if we scaled the game worldwide, and then further divided the workload into a long list of possible sub roles, so a player actually has a finite but challenging piece of a much larger conflict? Like a B52, where you have a pilot, co-pilot, navigator, gunner and bombsite operator?"

"But how in the world would we build a *global* virtual planet, something that seemed even remotely accurate? We don't have that kind of money."

Marc was ready to drop the final shoe, the one key element that pulled the whole idea together. "We don't have to build a virtual world. We already have a real digitized world. Actually, we have two." Dave stared back at Marc, his brow knitting in confusion. "Real world number one, Dave: Microsoft Flight Simulator. And to fill in any holes with that, we have real world number two, right here at Google, something you in particular are uniquely familiar with: Google Earth."

The pieces clicked into place for Dave that day. Two months later, Dave and Marc simultaneously announced their retirement from Google. Marc suggested that Dave should relocate to Austin with him, and to save money, Dave moved into an apartment with Marc and Elle. That is, until he convinced Julia to move out to Austin. They picked out an apartment just off South Congress

Avenue, and Dave fronted her the cash to open her own fashion boutique on SoCo just a few blocks south of Allen's Boots. Dave was covering the rent for both the apartment and the storefront, but it was a small price to pay to have Julia in his arms every night. Or at least every night he wasn't coding away on *Dronewars.*

Five thousand bucks apiece bought them a corporate business license, a preliminary company logo and a development server. Another twenty dollars a month got them a professional license for Lockheed Martin's Prepar3D software, a derivative of the original Microsoft Flight Simulator, plus a free copy of the software development kit for the simulator. While not the same as a source code license, it was a cheap way to get started implementing a proof of concept vehicle. A demo.

They also invested in a slightly used Xbox One, complete with Kinect, an extra controller and copies of the hottest new games. Neither of them had been serious gamers growing up — Dave, in particular, found writing code to be far more enjoyable than wasting time developing carpal tunnel problems and thumb blisters. But Marc's early research indicated that real gamers, the kind of gamers they were targeting, only played on dedicated game consoles. And the console of choice for war simulations was the Xbox.

Focusing on console-based development also solved other problems. Whereas PCs cover the full range of horsepower, memory and video resolutions, dedicated video consoles come in only one flavor. A flavor that beats all but the most expensive and exotic PCs hands down. All of that translated into a reliable, predictable gaming platform that had the power to handle *Dronewars'* massive storage and memory requirements.

But the one downside to console development was the staggering level of bureaucracy imposed by Microsoft on companies wanting access to the Xbox software development kit, what Microsoft calls "our rigorous qualification process." Early development and testing of the game was being done under Windows, but lack of access to the Xbox SDK meant Dave was falling further and further behind in getting up to speed on Xbox development. He assumed that, since Xbox was built on top of the DirectX video interface, the video function calls should be very similar to accessing DirectX under Windows. Still, knowing something in theory and testing it in practice are two very different things. Even more disconcerting was the fact that Microsoft had never ported Flight Simulator to the Xbox platform. There had to be a good reason for that, and Dave suspected that it was a reason that was going to rise up very soon and bite him in the ass.

None of this was a surprise. Dave had been fully aware of the challenges facing him when he walked into his boss's office at Google and handed over his resignation letter. And they didn't really worry him all that much — he had always been a boy wonder at Google, finding creative solutions to software problems everyone else had already bailed on.

But now the problem wasn't about coding, it was about access, access to the underlying Flight Simulator code and access to the Xbox software development kit. Dovetail had that access, had it

34

in spades, and in the days leading up to that lunch meeting with Dovetail in New York, Dave had known in his gut that some kind of relationship with Dovetail was essential to their success, essential to the very survival of Rocketship and the *Dronewars* project. All of his hopes for the future had been riding on that meeting.

So when Hal Porter suddenly stomped out of the restaurant, the last shred of hope still clinging to Dave's soul walked out with him.

9

As they left the restaurant and hailed a cab to LaGuardia, Marc knew that something was seriously wrong with Dave. After the lunches arrived, Marc had picked at his food, but Dave just stared at his plate, not eating a single bite. Marc kept trying to engage Dave in conversation, but it was like talking to a brick wall. The only response he got back was a barely perceptible shake of his head. Finally, since he didn't really have much of an appetite either, Marc signaled for the waitress, paid the bill, and headed outside. Dave followed silently behind.

The meeting with Dovetail had been shocking to Dave, in particular since it seemed so out of context with the emails they had exchanged with the company over the previous month. Nothing had prepared him for even the possibility of this kind of response. *If they had zero interest in working with us, why did they even agree to a meeting? Why waste their time and our money to have us fly all the way out to New York, just to tell us to get lost?* Something had to have changed at Dovetail. Maybe some internal battle, the usual company politics. That would explain why neither Jackson nor Gatland showed up as promised, but sent their lackeys instead. *But if they had changed their mind, if they just decided they weren't interested in working with us, they could have handled it a different way.* Dave was staring out the window of the cab but not seeing anything. *I mean, maybe we don't look like much right now, but they just firebombed a fucking bridge, a bridge that might actually mean*

36

something to them in the future. And after today, Dave couldn't imagine trusting them ever again. That bridge was gone.

But failing to land a deal with Dovetail wasn't the end of the world. It wasn't even all that surprising. When you got right down to it, Rocketship wasn't bringing very much to the table that Dovetail would want. Dave had counted on the Google glow to buy them some currency, some credibility, but at the end of the day he should have known that the deal really didn't make much sense for Dovetail. Or even for Rocketship, for that matter.

Dave was scarcely any better at the airport as they sat waiting for their flight. Marc grabbed a Starbucks and suggested shooting off an email to his contacts at Dovetail, but Dave thought better of it. It just looked too desperate, and besides, what good would ever come of it? What's done is done. It's over. Time to think about other options.

Marc scrolled down the list of emails that had come in over lunch. "Hey, Dave, we got a message from a guy at Microsoft Studios. They think they have a contact person for us over at Lockheed."

Dave didn't hold out much hope for Lockheed, which seemed like an even worse fit for Rocketship and *Dronewars* than Dovetail, but he couldn't very well ignore the offer for help from Microsoft. *We need those guys*, he thought. At the end of the day, all roads lead to Redmond. At least, all the roads Dave could foresee. *From the Google frying pan to the Microsoft fire. How did I not see this coming?*

37

The plane was starting to board, but since it was a day trip neither Marc nor Dave had any carryon bags, so neither of them were in a giant hurry to get onboard early. Marc gulped down the rest of his mocha latte and shot off a quick email to the guy at Lockheed.

10

Europe remained in the grip of one of the harshest winters in modern memory. Compounding the continent's misery, the Russian energy giant Gazprom cut off shipments of natural gas to Europe in retaliation for the October deployment of NATO's Very High Readiness Joint Task Force in the Baltic, the Western bloc's "Spearhead Force" intended to counter Russian aggression in the region. Since European gas exports accounted for almost all of Gazprom's foreign revenues, the Russian Ministry of Defense agreed to compensate the company for its lost profits, gambling that a gas boycott had a greater chance of success against NATO than a head-to-head military confrontation with the West.

The gamble paid off. Faced with soaring casualties from the cold and a potentially devastating depression, and with energy-starved factories now idled across the continent, the European leadership blinked. The VJTF was recalled and disbanded, its troops and equipment blended back into other NATO units. Almost immediately, stripped of their NATO security blanket and feeling abandoned by their Western European allies, the former Soviet bloc countries of Eastern and Central Europe signaled they were finally ready to negotiate for closer ties to the Russian Federation.

11

Dave remained in a funk over the weekend, avoiding the office apartment for long walks along the hike and bike trail at Lady Bird Lake. He had already hit the wall as far as development went — while he had worked minor miracles building aircraft and combat scenarios with the Prepar3D software development kit, at this point he couldn't move much further ahead without the source code. Marc held out hope that Lockheed might be willing to hand over their copy of the code, along with the significant enhancements to the original Flight Simulator X software they'd made in the interim, but Dave didn't share his enthusiasm. Lockheed was a *defense contractor*, for God's sake. Why in the world would they want to get in bed with a video game company?

Not for the first time, Dave wished he had been able to make it to the demo at CES, just to get his own take on what really went down, his own gut feel for whether the MS Studios guys had any real interest in the project. Marc just couldn't be trusted. Not that he would lie, it's just that he always seemed to see the glass as half full. And Dave was a glass half empty kind of guy. The world was full of fewer surprises that way.

The mid-January air was crisp, but the sun felt good, and the bright blue Texas skies helped to soften his mood. Marc still hadn't heard back from the guy at Lockheed, which wasn't all that surprising. Deep down, Dave wished Lockheed would just blow them off, not dangle something shiny in front of them that ultimately they had no intention of sharing. And why would they? Lockheed was a military contractor, and Prepar3D was primarily just a vehicle for military training.

As late as the 1970's, flight simulators were considered nothing more than games. Part of that was due to the lack of realistic computer graphics — at a time when *Pong* was the ultimate achievement in computer user interface design, a computer-based flight simulator was simply not an option. All that began to change in the 1980's, when computer displays shifted from green-on-black character displays to higher and higher resolution graphical displays. In 1985, Microprose released *F15 Strike Eagle*, a combat flight simulator that sold well over 1.5 million copies and was voted Action Game of the Year in Computer Gaming World's 1985 reader poll. Five years later, Origin Systems launched *Wing Commander*, a science fiction space combat simulation with breakthrough graphics and absorbing game play. Computer Gaming World's readers gave *Wing Commander* a score of 10.91, the highest rating ever for a video game. Until it was ultimately dethroned by *Wing Commander II*.

The first version of *Microsoft Flight Simulator* was launched in 1982, three years before the release of the first version of Microsoft Windows. It was intended to be a tour-de-force for the IBM PC and similar 16-bit personal computers, demonstrating the greatly enhanced power and graphics capabilities of the newest generation of computers. While the first versions sported very primitive and unrealistic graphics, by the late 1980's the game began to feature 3D graphics and hardware-based graphic acceleration. The increased realism and low cost of *Flight Simulator* made it a quick favorite of the private pilot community, particularly when the software was combined with realistic flight yokes and pedals, giving beginning pilots a cheaper (and safer) way to learn how to fly.

The Federal Aviation Administration refused to certify the consumer version of *Flight Simulator* for aviation training, so none of the hours spent inside the virtual cockpit could be counted toward a pilot's license. But other companies quickly stepped into that void with commercial flight simulators that FAA ultimately approved for training.

None of this escaped the attention of the airline industry and the United States Department of Defense, both of which quickly adopted flight simulators as a mandatory part of their pilot training programs. The benefits of flight simulators over training in actual aircraft were enormous. First of all, given the high cost of operations for commercial and military aircraft, a high-quality flight simulator could pay for itself in just a few virtual flights. Second was the issue of safety, not just for the pilot in training but also potentially for the passengers of a commercial aviation jet or the crew of a military aircraft. Not to mention the cost of the planes involved. Finally, flight simulators let pilots train for in-flight emergencies and scenarios that would otherwise be impossible to simulate in an actual aircraft. Toss a flock of geese into the engines of a 737 taking off from JFK and let a pilot experience a *real* emergency with zero downside. Repeat ad nauseam until her response to the emergency proved to be instantaneous and nearly perfect.

Studies funded by the United States Air Force showed that almost all casualties in aerial combat were experienced by low-time pilots. Flight simulators were able to minimize the mistakes made by those pilots, making budding warriors far more proficient and deadly in the air. Ultimately, the other armed services started taking notice, as well, particularly as the fire control systems for tanks and warships became more and more sophisticated, and the differences between video games and real weapons began to blur. That line between the real and the virtual became almost nonexistent when the CIA and the Air Force began their drone warfare campaigns in the Middle East as part of President Bush's "War on Terror" in Afghanistan, Pakistan and Iraq. In fact, by 2012 the USAF was training more pilots for its "Remote Piloted Vehicles" than for ordinary jet fighter aircraft.

Most of the flight simulators acquired by the various branches of the military were specific to each type of airplane. But in contrast, most of the pilot training was more generic in nature, and DOD finally put out a request for a new type of simulator that could be cheaply modified for a variety of aircraft, tanks and sea craft.

Meanwhile, Microsoft was beginning to rethink its commitment to *Flight Simulator*. Once the darling of Wall Street, the company was starting to show its age. Revenues and profits were slowing, particularly for the core Windows and Office franchises, and there was no clear vision of what new products or markets would drive their future growth. Once a leader in smart phone and tablet technologies, Microsoft was rapidly falling behind rivals Google and Apple. Even Internet Explorer was being pushed aside by the newly launched Google Chrome browser. Steve Ballmer, fully in control at Microsoft when Bill Gates pulled back from day-to-day management in 2006, decided that the company needed to focus its attention on the new product threats and eliminate any distractions. As a result, in January 2009, amid other widespread job cuts at Microsoft, it was announced that Aces Studio — the team responsible for development and marketing of *Flight Simulator* — had been shuttered.

Ultimately, the increasing realism of *Flight Simulator* proved its undoing, as realism translated into increasing complexity and decreasing playability. In the end it was just a simulator, not a game, and while pilots greatly appreciated the more than 24,000 airports, real-time weather, programmable in-flight failures and air traffic control simulations, gamers just wanted to shoot things down and blow things up. Simulating a five-hour flight from LAX to Las Vegas McCarran just wasn't any *fun*.

With Aces Studio in ashes and the entire *Flight Simulator* team laid off, Microsoft licensed the rights and source code for the commercial simulator version of the program to Lockheed Martin. Lockheed soon announced a rebranding of the software as Prepar3D (pronounced *prepared*), and hired several members of the old Aces development team to continue development of the product. In 2014, Dovetail Games, based in Chatham, Kent, announced that they had licensed the rights to the consumer version of *Flight Simulator*, and launched *Microsoft Flight Simulator X: Steam Edition* the next December.

So the question that kept bugging Dave was: why would Lockheed waste any time on a startup game developer if their core focus was the high-dollar military market? With Dovetail out of the picture, that left only Microsoft Studios, and they were notoriously slow to move on anything. Sony was always an option with the PS4 development kit that they seemed eager to just give away to any game developer who could fog a mirror, but that still didn't address the question of the flight sim source code. Or the rich flight sim geographic database.

Dave had been walking in his own mental fog along the south shore of the lake when suddenly a large black dog darted out of the bushes right in front of him. Startled, he stopped, glanced up, and found himself face-to-face with Stevie Ray Vaughan. Or, more accurately, the statue of Stevie Ray Vaughan that had been placed on the south shore jogging path to commemorate the life of the famous musician, who died in a helicopter accident near Chicago at the age of 35. Cut down at the peak of his career.

Vaughan was an icon of the Austin live music scene, a musician who had cut his chops in all the local dives and hangouts well before he suddenly arrived as a breakout blues star. Addicted to alcohol and drugs from a very early age, Vaughan had broken free of those monkeys in the last years of his life, and was finally living a complete and happy existence when his Bell 206B Jet Ranger helicopter, rising up through a bank of low-lying clouds, crashed into the side of a 300-foot-tall ski mountain. The helicopter had missed clearing the mountain by only fifty feet.

As Dave stood staring at the bronze Vaughan, blazing in the golden firelight from the sun now settling in the western sky, he felt another fire begin to stir, a fire that had been ebbing away over the past several months, a fire almost snuffed out by the meeting with Dovetail. "Well, my friend, you may have died young, but you died full of life," he murmured aloud. "With so much working against you, you somehow fought through all of it and finally found true happiness. Finally found peace."

Turning slowly to watch as the sun swelled red across the lake, Dave decided it was time to seek his own kind of peace. And he knew just where that search would begin. He tapped at the screen of his smart watch. "Dial Jules," he ordered, pulling his phone from his back pocket. He'd ignored her long enough, he thought. And in the process had almost lost her. Tonight all of that would change.

to the stars

12

S anders stared out the window of his apartment, lost in thought. Just across the Potomac River he could make out the back of the Lincoln Memorial, and beyond that the unmistakable white spire of the Washington Monument. Today he felt older than either of them.

It just wasn't fair. He had given everything he had for this country, and it still kept coming back, demanding even more. But deep in his heart he knew that a never ending sacrifice was just part of the job description, part of the oath he had given when he took the job. And he knew full well that this was nothing compared to the sacrifice millions of other men and women had made over the last two and a half centuries to keep this country free. Many of them laid to rest just off to his right in Arlington National Cemetery.

Sanders was also acutely aware that he could have easily ended all of this by simply voting no to the tie score. A simple no and she would have been right back here with him, right back here lying in the bed behind him. No one would have questioned him, no one would have thought twice about his commitment.

He stared down at the thick report he held in his hands, a report full of nothing but bad news, news he was scheduled to deliver in person to the president early the next morning. America was spending more on its military each year than all of the other nations in the world combined, and yet, in situation after situation, it seemed that the red white and blue was always on its heels. Always on the losing end of things.

The core problem was that the military was spread way too thin, scattered across the globe in hunkered down, defensive positions. It was like keeping a dog on a leash — anyone who knew the length of that leash or was willing to test the edges of it could rape and plunder at will. As a result, America's enemies could simply pick their fights, probe the front lines for isolated areas of relative weakness to exploit. Like Russia's brazen seizure of Crimea.

Problem number two was the country's role in establishing and defending morality and humanity in global affairs, in insisting upon the primacy of the rule of law. The country that had had its moral hands bloodied by Hiroshima and Nagasaki could now only watch and condemn as other global actors violated international standards and prohibitions at will. And laughed in America's face all the while they were doing so.

Finally, problem number three was America's predictability. By pressing for sanctions and other diplomatic efforts to rein in countries like Iran and North Korea, and then limiting any real military action to "measured and proportional" attacks, Uncle Sam's massive military capabilities were largely kept at bay. On a leash. The country had effectively neutered itself on the world stage.

Sanders knew all of this, had lived it all on a daily basis for over three decades. And as he held the report in his hands, it wasn't the weight of the report itself that bothered him so much. It was the weight of what it represented. A weight that increasingly he alone bore.

There was no longer anything his country could do about problem number one — America had bought its footholds around the world at a heavy price, and simply abandoning those frontline positions to the enemy, just walking away and retreating back to her home shores, was not an option.

And problem number two was off the table as well. The horrors of World Wars I and II, all of the precious lives that had been lost over the first half of the twentieth century, from the poison gas used in trench warfare to the ovens of Auschwitz and Treblinka to the devastating pogroms of Stalin's Soviet Russia — the price of progress in human affairs was just too great to calculate, and any surrender to the forces of darkness would be too great an insult to those who had bought that progress with their own precious blood.

So that left problem number three. Predictability.

13

The night air had turned far too chilly to sit outside at Justine's, and inside was always too crowded and way too loud, so Dave decided instead to try Foreign and Domestic in North Hyde Park. The food was always good, if a bit too exotic for some people's tastes, and Dave loved the simple feel of the place and the fact that he could watch the food being prepared in the open kitchen. He and Julia grabbed a two-seater near the back corner.

When the waitress strolled over, Dave ordered a Buried Hatchet Stout from Southern Star Brewing, a craft brewer out of Conroe, Texas. Julia as usual ordered a chardonnay. *You can take the girl out of California...* he chuckled to himself.

Julia was looking radiant, as usual. She was dressed in an off-white silk blouse, her auburn curls falling in waves around her shoulders. Her skirt was navy tulle, cut fashionably short and spreading out in a wide V from her impossibly narrow waist. Dave hadn't changed from his walk along the lake, and was still wearing jeans and a faded blue Captain America tee.

"It's great to get out of SoCo for a change, Dave. Thanks for picking this place." The good Austin restaurants were always crowded, even on a Sunday night, but Foreign and Domestic had a limited reservations policy, so it was usually a good choice for a last-minute drop-in.

"Thanks for putting up with me, Jules," Dave replied, clinking his stout against her upraised wine glass. "I've been kind of an ass, particularly since we got back from New York, and I think it's time I made it up to you."

Julia shook her head like it didn't matter, but Dave knew better. "Oh, sweetie, I know you've been killing yourself to get the program ready for that show. I understood that when I moved out here. I've just been kinda missing your sweet company. You're pretty much all I've got going out here."

That wasn't exactly true. When Dave finally convinced Julia to join him in Austin, he knew he had to find something to keep her occupied, something productive that would make it less obvious that she was basically his kept woman, a status she would have never tolerated. Julia Adams had a degree in graphics design, a field that had left her grossly underemployed in the Bay Area, but her real heart was in fashion, so Dave helped her set up a small dress shop in SoCo. "Jules." Officially it was just an investment, and Dave had paid a lawyer friend to draw up the paperwork to make it clear he was a minority partner, but in reality he just saw it as a shiny new toy to keep Julia busy. Surprisingly, she was actually making a go of it, specializing in forward-looking women's styles that featured young designers from the Austin metro area. *Jules* was quickly becoming a big hit with the hip and increasingly rich young crowd that was transforming the once-sleepy college town into a Mecca for high tech and music. And all that meant more free time for Dave to pound out code.

But that was all about to change. Dave now realized that since leaving Google and moving to Austin, he had lost his work-life balance, and in the process had lost perspective on what was really important to him. *Too much work and no play makes Davy a dull boy.* He didn't miss the BMW, and after seeing the sorry state of Austin's streets he knew that the 18-inch rims wouldn't have lasted a month, anyway, but he missed showing Julia off at plays and art shows and concerts around San Francisco. Of course, Austin had all of that, in spades, plus the music scene and ACL Fest and the SXSW music festival... *oh crap, that's just two months away!* He looked up again at Julia's impossibly blue eyes. *Well, I'll worry about that tomorrow*, he decided, smiling back at her and sipping on his beer.

"Davy, you know that Dallas Fashion Week is coming up in March, and we're going to have a small booth up there to show off our new designs. I'd love to have you join me. We could get a room at the Hyatt, grab dinner at The French Room and Scardello." She paused seductively. "I could buy a *special outfit* for the occasion."

Shit. I forgot all about that. Fashion Week in Dallas is the very same week as the SXSW Gaming Expo. I can't afford to miss that — Marc would kill me. "Uh, I think I might have a conflict—" Julia glanced down, but not before he noticed the disappointment lingering in her eyes. Just one more disappointment in a long series of screw-ups on his part. "Look, we have a major gaming conference here in Austin at the same time, and I can't miss it, but Love Field is not far from the Hyatt. I can do the conference here during the day and catch a flight up to Dallas in the late afternoon every day and be there for you every night. It'll work out great. You'll be so busy in the booth you'll never miss me, and I won't have to sit around in the hotel every day waiting for you to get finished with your work."

"You'd do that for me? Oh, Davy, thank you, thank you, thank you! It'll be *so* much fun, I promise!" Her smile was the best thank you Julia could have possibly given him. Dave would work it all out tomorrow with Marc. Heck, maybe Elle would like to take a break and help Julia out with the booth. Marc could join them all in Dallas for one or two nights, depending upon what was scheduled for the SXSW evening sessions.

The waitress joined them to take their order, and Dave splurged on the buttermilk biscuit stuffed quail, with Julia opting for the vegetarian corn & chanterelle risotto. *This is going to be a really good night for a change*, he thought, smiling across the table at the most wonderful thing that had ever come into his life.

14

H ey, buddy, no worries," Marc reassured him. "I just got the proposed schedule for the conference, and there isn't much going on that you need to see, anyway, particularly the evening sessions. I can cover all those for you. And I'm having lunch with Elle today, so I'll hit her up about helping Julia out with the booth."

Marc was just glad to see his partner back in good spirits. "In fact, you remember Jack Travers? He's got a Piper stashed out at Lakeway, and he's always trying to find a good excuse to take it out on a mission. You cover his avgas and I'm sure he'd love to ferry you back and forth to Dallas."

"That's a great idea, Marc. A lot more flexibility with the time, and the way that plane sips gas, probably a lot cheaper for me than Southwest."

"Plus you skip security," Marc added.

"Yeah, plus that. I can wait and get my pat-downs from Jules when I get to Dallas," Dave chuckled. "By the way, any word from Orlando?" Lockheed's Prepar3D team was headquartered in Orlando, Florida.

"Nah, but I'm not surprised. You know those corporate types. Probably pass it on to some lackey, who'll pass it on to his lackey, and maybe we'll hear back in a few weeks."

"Well, I'm hoping its sooner rather than later," Dave replied. "Without the source code or Xbox SDK, I'm kind of running out of things to do. I was thinking last night about nabbing a PS4 developer's kit, just to start getting a handle on what coding on a game console looks like. They can't be all that different."

"Not a bad idea, " Marc offered. "Plus it might help you to keep cross-platform compatibility in mind when you finally start working on the Xbox port, just in case we decide to expand to Sony at some point in the future."

"Okay, I'll get right on that. It'll mean springing for another console, but it beats just sitting around and watching the grass grow. Or helping Jules out with the shop." Dave faked a pain in his stomach.

"Yeah, like you'd ever complain about sitting around and staring at Julia like a starry-eyed schoolboy," Marc laughed, grabbing a Topo Chico from the fridge and popping it open with the bottle opener attached to his key chain. "By the way, I have a conference call this afternoon with some of the guys from MS Studios. They have some questions about our Xbox SDK application we need to clear up. You got time to sit in?"

"All the time in the world. Where are you meeting Elle?" Dave leaned over and pulled up the Sony PS4 developer's page on his laptop screen:

Before applying, please make sure the following requirements are met:

- *Proof of Corporate Entity*

- *Obtain an Employer Tax ID Number (see www.irs.gov) (Recommended)*
- *Static IP to access Developer Support Systems*
- *You must be physically located in US, Mexico, Central America, South America, or Canada*

"Check, check, check and check. Well, that's a relief. Looks like we qualify," Dave chortled as he clicked the orange 'Get Started' button. The screen changed to PlayStation Partner Registration, and Dave scrolled down to the application form. "Hey, bro, they're asking for a PDF of our Certificate of Formation. Know where that might be stashed?"

"Sure. It's on Dropbox, under Corporate, Legal, Inc Docs," Marc answered.

"Got it. Wow, this is pretty damned easy. Too bad Sony doesn't have a flight sim." Dave's fingers danced on the keyboard, and in less than a minute clicked 'Confirm' to send the application on its way. "Doesn't say we need a console, but I'll take that as a given," Dave noted as he quickly checked PS4 pricing on Amazon and eBay. "Do you care if it's used? I can grab a one terabyte unit with Call of Duty Black Ops for under three hundred."

"Have at it. Maybe when you're finished with it we can gift it to some charity for pimply-faced virgin boys," Marc smiled.

"Watch yourself, my friend. Some of us still haven't recovered from those days, " Dave countered playfully.

"Hey, I've seen Julia in a bathing suit. Believe me, you've recovered." Marc was still laughing as he headed out the door for his lunch with Elle.

15

W hat day did you say that was?" Elle asked, checking her calendar.

"Starts March 16, which I believe is a Thursday." Marc had agreed to meet her at Madam Mam's, a Thai restaurant on the Drag across from the University of Texas campus. Street parking was tight around campus, so he had parked in the UT Coop garage and walked over. He planned to drop in to the Coop basement after lunch to pick up a copy of the textbook for the video game marketing class at the McCombs School, so he'd get his parking ticket stamped for free.

"That would work," Elle told him, already entering the dates into her phone. "Actually, it will give me kind of a head start on spring break, which also starts that weekend."

"Wouldn't want to be the cause of you missing some sun time down in Cancun," Marc teased.

"Just take one look at this alabaster skin. Do you think this skin has ever seen the Mexican sun?" Elle was blessed with the kind of creamy white skin only a true redhead could pull off. "Besides, it'll be good to get in some girl time with Jules. Compare notes. Figure out our next big boyfriend moves."

"Ouch! That sounds like a *really* bad idea."

"Well, then, watch yourself, buster. You have been officially warned." Elle's green eyes twinkled. The threat of dumping Marc had been a long-running joke between them.

"Duly noted. So it's settled, then. I'll take care of all the arrangements." The waitress arrived with their plates, and Marc moved his Thai coffee to make room. "Oh, one other thing, I think Julia wants to go down on Wednesday to make sure everything is set up right. Okay if I put you guys up together in one room on Wednesday night, then move you to your own room on Thursday?"

Elle glanced up at him with a sly smile. "What happens if Jules and I get lucky and find some big city boys to bring back to the room? That might get a little awkward."

Marc smirked back. "Yeah, well, alls I'm sayin' is, if some slick Dallas boy wants to sweet-talk his way into your panties, it won't be on my dime."

"Fair enough. His apartment is way more comfortable, anyway," Elle countered, digging into her plate of Guay Teaw Kua Gai with relish.

"Hey!" Marc grabbed at his chest like he'd been shot by an arrow, and Elle giggled so hard she choked on her bite.

"Actually, skipping class on Thursday is not really a problem," Elle suggested. "We have Fridays off, and all I've got on Thursdays is cost accounting. This gives me a perfect excuse to skip it for once." Cost accounting was a core class in the MBA program, one every student was required to take. But Elle's interests lay in marketing and entrepreneurship, and although — technically speaking — marketing included figuring out the cost of goods, the subject was just so *boring*. "I'm done on Wednesday around three, so Julia and I can head up any time she's ready."

Just then Marc's watch buzzed. He pushed his sleeve back and saw he had just gotten an email back from Lockheed. Tapping the watch face, he quickly scrolled through the message.

"What, getting text messages from your other honey while you're on a date with *me*? That is so *wrong*."

Marc laughed. "Actually, hon, it's from Lockheed. They want to meet with us next week." Marc pulled out his phone to check the message on the bigger screen. Sometimes details got lost trying to read emails on his smartwatch, but more than that he was just so excited. He needed more confirmation that the meet with Lockheed was really on.

Elle's eyes lit up. She knew how disappointed the boys had been from their disaster in New York, even though Marc had tried very hard not to show it. For Lockheed to respond this quickly to Marc's email on Friday was a good indication that they might be very interested. And she was under no illusions as to what that really meant. "When do they suggest you head out there?"

"They say Wednesday and Thursday are free, so either day. They also suggested we get there the night before, so we can have plenty of time to run through the demo the next morning and dig into whether there's a good fit between us." Marc was cautiously excited. He was fully aware of the issues with Lockheed, but their quick turn-around on his email plus the amount of time they had blocked out for the meeting was a *very* good sign. He punched up Dave's number on his phone.

"Hey, Dave. Great news! Lockheed wants to meet with us next week!" Marc couldn't keep the enthusiasm from showing in his voice.

"Wow! That was quick."

"I know! They're suggesting Wednesday or Thursday, get there the night before so we can make an early morning meeting. I'm thinking we go out Wednesday night, so we don't look overly eager.—" Marc was grinning ear-to-ear. Elle reached across the table to grab his hand, happy to see him so excited.

"R-i-i-i-ight," Dave drawled back. "While we're at it, why don't we just tell'em we're kinda busy and we'll catch up with them next month?"

"That's a great idea, Dave, but my next month is really booked. What say we just check into flights for Tuesday. That way I won't have to miss my Wednesday night poker game." Marc winked at Elle.

"Hey, we can cover the cost of the trip in what you don't lose playing poker!" Dave laughed. Marc was actually a pretty good poker player. He had a natural liar's face, completely unreadable, and a bold willingness to bluff regardless of what was showing in his hand. Dave had long since refused to play with him.

"Tuesday it is, then. I'll pop an email back to them and work out the details. Oh, and Elle says she's on for Dallas."

"Well, this is turning into a pretty good Monday. I'll get Jules into the loop about Dallas, and just so you know, everything up there is on me. We'll call it all a tax write-off for Jules' shop."

63

"That works for me, buddy. See ya in a few." Marc hung up and quickly started composing a reply for Lockheed.

"Speaking of over-eager, don't you think that can wait until after lunch?" Elle reminded him, nodding at the cooling plate of curry sitting in front of him.

"Uh, yeah. You're right. And this really does smell pretty good." Marc tucked into his dish with renewed relish, while Elle just sat back for a moment and smiled. Things were finally starting to fall into place. Just like they'd planned.

16

The week leading up to the meeting in Orlando was nerve-wracking, with both boys trying to stay busy to keep Lockheed off their minds. Dave had hunted down an old college friend at Electronic Arts who sent him a copy of the PS4 software development kit, the SDK, and he was already diving deep into the documentation and sample code. Dave had asked about getting his hands on the Xbox SDK, as well, but his friend thought that might be a problem. Since Sony was essentially making the PS4 kit available to almost anyone, and since Dave had already applied to Sony for developer status, getting a jump on the Sony SDK wouldn't raise any red flags. But Microsoft was known to be hard-ass about its non-disclosures, and Dave's friend didn't want to lose his job at EA by doing favors for old buddies.

While the Sony SDK was useful for helping Dave get his head around coding for game consoles, he didn't have a Sony SDK login, so he didn't have access to any of the online resources Sony provided for its developer community. Dave was pretty sure the real meat behind programming the PS4 would be on those blogs and websites, and he could hardly wait to get his final approval from Sony so he could dive in more fully.

Meanwhile, Marc was swamped trying to put together a business plan and pro forma financials for *Dronewars*. Microsoft had indicated they needed a completed plan and projected sales numbers before they could move further with the developer application, and the back-of-the-envelope planning Marc and Dave had done months earlier didn't count. Elle was helping out with the Excel analysis, so Marc could focus more on fluffing up the business plan.

Elle's fledgling business training was proving to be a godsend. She had pulled up a sample business plan and pro formas for a similar project from the Internet, and the two were using it as a template for Rocketship. But the deeper they got into the numbers, the more Marc got concerned. He had started to realize that he had been amazingly naive about the costs associated with launching an Xbox game, particularly the unavoidable packaging and advertising costs for launch, which were astronomical.

While many new game developers had moved to on-line distribution, where buyers simply downloaded the games and documentation over the Internet, the code and geo database for *Dronewars* were way too large for electronic distribution. In fact, Dave was suggesting that even DVDs might be too small to be practical — they would need to go to Blu-Ray or the newer 4k HD disks, and deal with backward compatibility issues on older consoles.

The template Elle had found suggested a minimum unit cost of around eight dollars per game. Given that there are over 4,000 Walmarts in the United States alone (not including Sam's Club stores and Walmart Express), with a stocking of five units per store, that added up to a minimum of $160,000 in game packaging costs for launch. Just for *Walmart*, not including Target, Best Buy, and all the

66

other game outlets across the country. The total cost of stocking for launch could easily exceed a million dollars.

And the cost of advertising was potentially several times that number. One full-page color ad running six times in just one gamer magazine, gameinformer, could cost well over $1.3 million.

Marc was stunned. "Elle, we just don't have that kind of money. I mean, we could come up with it, but if the game tanks, Dave and I would be ruined!"

Elle frowned, nodding her head in agreement. "Well, we still need to nail these numbers down, but you're right, if these are correct, it's a real game changer for us. Literally."

"On the production cost side," Marc suggested, "wouldn't those be offset by order revenue? The stores are buying from us, right? So it's really just a matter of fronting the cash for a month or so and getting it back when we ship, plus profits."

Elle shook her head. "Maybe for an established gaming house, but unless we get Microsoft to bless us somehow, my best guess is the stores will effectively take the games on consignment, delaying payment to see how well they sell, and then returning the games to us if they don't. Or, since we would have like zero use for a pile of returned games, get us to write off what they owe us and just stick them in the dollar pile to get rid of them."

Her eyes took on a faraway look as she sorted through other options. "You know, have you ever considered a Kickstarter campaign? We could offer the game for free to anyone who fronts, say, ten bucks or twenty bucks. Or maybe ten bucks for an early release version. That would also help build early buzz for the game with dedicated gamers, which could also kickstart the marketing, so to speak. And an early release would give us some great feedback on what folks think is working and what things we need to fix."

"That's a great idea, Elle! We can kill two birds with one throw." Marc's use of the idiom wasn't exactly right, but Elle wasn't going to correct him. He had a habit of mashing up the English language, like when he called window sills "seals," and Elle had just learned to take all that as an adorable little quirk.

Marc pulled up some examples of successful crowd-funded campaigns on his laptop, and they quickly dived into coming up with ideas for how it might all come together. Putting together a business plan had turned out to be much more work than they had originally budgeted, but it had the unexpected side benefit of highlighting some problems they hadn't even thought existed, and forcing them to dig deeper into what it would take to get the product out the door and into the hands of their target customers. A hole that increasingly seemed to be almost bottomless.

17

The flight into Orlando was uneventful, and, getting in very late at night, Marc and Dave were glad that they had decided to stay in the Hyatt located inside the airport. They had booked just one room with two queen beds to save some cash, and they quickly dropped their bags off in the room and headed downstairs for dinner.

It was too late for the main restaurant, but McCoy's Bar and Grill was still open, so they grabbed a spot at the end of the communal table. The waitress handed them each a Late Night Menu and suggested they try some of the small plates options. Dave scanned it quickly and ordered the fish and chips with malt vinegar. Marc went for the Cuban sandwich, and they both opted for a glass of the Gina Kogen Japanese craft beer.

After dinner they unpacked, and Marc showed Dave how to hang his shirt and sport jacket in the shower and run the hot water so the steam would ease out any wrinkles. Dave ran through the demo one last time to make sure everything was still working perfectly, then plugged in his laptop, phone and watch, turning the watch face so he could make out the time in barely glowing blue numbers in the darkened room. Marc plugged his electronics in, as well, set an alarm on his phone for the morning, then called in a backup alarm to the front desk.

"See ya at the crack of dawn, Dave," Marc called out, turning off the bedside light.

"Hey, watch that crack of yours," Dave answered, pulling the sheets up to his chin and rolling over on his side. "If you're sleeping in the nude again I'm getting another room!"

Marc shook his head but was way too tired to respond, and soon they were both fast asleep.

18

Morning came all too early, and Marc swore at the cheerful tone of the alarm he had set the night before. He crawled out of bed, stumbling across the room in his boxer underwear to start the in-room coffee before heading toward the toilet. Dave rubbed his eyes, looking over at the time, then flicked on the bedside light and slowly rose up out of bed. He noticed that the coffee had been started, and Marc was still in the bathroom, so he shuffled to the door to pick up the morning's complimentary copy of USA Today. Complimentary, he thought, as long as you're willing to blow two hundred bucks on the room.

Marc emerged from the bathroom. "Want me to pour you some coffee, Dave?" he asked, pulling apart the paper coffee cups on the counter.

"That depends upon whether you washed your hands after peeing," Dave grumbled, heading into the bathroom himself. Marc didn't answer, but when Dave was finished in the bathroom he noticed a steaming cup of coffee sitting next to his watch on the bed stand. He walked over and grabbed a quick sip, insipidly weak but still better than nothing at this hour.

Marc was sitting on his bed, pulling on a shirt and pants. "Why don't we head down for breakfast before getting dolled up for the meeting," he suggested, hunting around for where he'd dropped his socks the night before.

"Sure. But you go on ahead. I need a quick shower just to wake up."

"Okay, but don't dawdle. The Lockheed guy is going to meet us downstairs in a little over an hour, and we don't want to be late." Marc slipped on his shoes, picked his room key up off the dresser and headed for the door as Dave pulled his toiletry bag out of his suitcase and aimed for the shower.

An hour later they were fully dressed, packed and checking out at the hotel front desk. Both were in jackets and ties — Marc had forgotten to verify the dress code for the meeting, but he surmised that, since Lockheed was primarily a military contractor, they would all be dressed in starched shirts and spit-polish shines.

"Actually, sir, you're all paid up," the lady at the counter was telling Marc. "Looks like Lockheed put it on their corporate account."

"How about dinner last night, and breakfast?" Mark asked.

"That, too, sir. All paid up. By the way, will you be flying out of Orlando later today? We'd be happy to keep your bags in the meantime, and you can pick them up later on today before you head for your flight."

Marc quickly checked the young lady's name tag. "Hey, that sounds great. Thanks, Cecilia." He flashed her a big smile as she motioned for the check room attendant.

"Damn nice of those Lockheed guys," Dave muttered to Marc. "Different world from what we saw in New York."

"Well, I'm sure they've got a lot of Defense Department money to spend, but I agree, so far they seem like a real class organization."

As the attendant was handing Marc the claim stubs for their luggage, a smartly dressed man with what looked like a military-issue haircut stepped up and stuck out his hand. "Hi, I'm Joe McAdams. And you guys are Marc Cullen and Dave Elliott, right?"

Dave was closest and quickly returned the handshake. "Yep, I'm Dave, nice to meet you."

"I see the hotel is storing your bags. Do you have anything else I can help you with?"

"No," Marc answered, "just our laptops for the demo."

"Great, in that case, follow me. The limo is pretty close by." McAdams spun and started out of the hotel at a brisk pace, Marc and Dave tucked in close behind.

The ride to Lockheed took just over twenty-five minutes. Dave was confused at first when the driver turned west on the Martin Anderson Beachline Expressway instead of east.

"Hey, isn't Lockheed up north?" He checked his phone. "Their web page says they're at 100 Global Innovation Circle. I tried Google maps and couldn't find that address, but the zip code says it's somewhere north and east of the airport."

"I don't know anything about that," the driver replied, glancing back at Dave in the rear view mirror. "I just know I was told to take you to Sand Lake."

Dave and Marc looked over at McAdams, seated across from them in the limo, who jumped in to explain. "We have some offices over at the old Global Innovation site, but that's mainly for sales and sales support. Our main offices are at Sand Lake, which is the primary Orlando facility for Lockheed. That's one of the reasons for the limo and the personal escort. Sand Lake is a secure site, so I'll need to walk you through security and to pick up your badges. If you had come over in a rental it might have taken half the morning just to get past the gates and the front door."

"Yeah, Google had some of the same problems," Marc noted. "Mostly people just wanting to get a look-see, or sneak into one of our restaurants on campus. It got really bad after that Internship movie came out with Vince Vaughn and Owen Wilson."

"Never heard of them. But I don't get out to many movies, anyway. I stick to mostly Clancy, stuff I can relate to. To be frank, I have access to some pretty interesting classified video, so I kinda prefer the real thing over some fake Hollywood version." McAdams had a big and friendly smile on his face, but it was clear he wasn't all that interested in video games, so Marc and Dave decided to finish the rest of the ride in silence.

Before long they pulled up to the Sand Lake facility, which appeared to be mostly two large white stone and black glass office buildings, one up front set in a large parking lot, and another slightly behind and to the right. The limo passed through the security gate without slowing and pulled up in front of the first building.

"Here we are, gentlemen," McAdams drawled, moving toward the car door as the driver ran around the back of the limo to open it. Marc and Dave followed McAdams out of the car and in through the front door, where another security station blocked their entrance. McAdams flashed a badge. "Elliott and Cullen. They're on the list," he barked at the security guard, who quickly checked his screen and waved them through. "Badges over there," the guard noted, pointing to a small table off to the left where a bored female attendant sat behind a digital ID camera.

"You first, Elliott. Stand on the white line, stare at the camera and look pretty," McAdams ordered, handing a sheet of paper to the camera attendant. Within a minute they each had a temporary paper ID, which they dutifully inserted into the plastic badge holder McAdams pointed to on the table, and then they were off down the labyrinthine halls of the Lockheed complex.

Several dozen turns and an elevator ride later, McAdams pointed toward an open doorway to their right. Marc was thoroughly lost, and suspected that it was actually all just part of the plan. McAdams held back and waved them through the door.

The conference room was fairly generic, a large rectangular table surrounded by about ten or so chairs, with more chairs pushed up against the walls. *Seating for the underlings*, Marc surmised. Just inside the door and to the left was a narrow table held down by a coffee pot, cups, creamers and sweeteners, and a large plate of bagels with a generous container of softened cream cheese. He quickly scanned the six people already seated around the table, and was surprised to see that none of them were wearing jackets or ties. The two younger guys closest to him were in T-shirts and jeans, the rest in collared polo shirts and slacks.

An impressively muscled man at the head of the table stood up to greet them. "Good morning, gentlemen. You must be Mr. Cullen and Mr. Elliott. I'm Bob Sanders. You can call me Bob. You and I have been exchanging emails, Mr. Cullen."

Marc nodded back in reply. "And it's just Marc and Dave." Despite his casual attire, everything else about Sanders screamed *military*. Close cropped hair, square jaw, a stiff, vertical posture. Like he had a parade baton stuck up his ass.

"Right. Informal it is. And, along those lines, it's clear you didn't get the memo about our dress code around here. I'm sorry about that. We try to avoid those damned hangman's nooses every chance we get, so it's generally business casual around here unless the brass is snooping around. Then we pull out the jackets and ties from the broom closet and try our damnedest to act like they aren't chafing our necks. You can pull those off and get comfortable if you'd like." Sanders motioned for them to grab a seat.

Marc pulled out a chair for Dave and sat down himself. "If you don't mind, we'll leave them on. It's the only jacket and tie I own," Marc lied, "and I'm afraid if I take them off I'll lose them and won't have anything left to get buried in."

"Good plan," Sanders chuckled. "By the way, if you're hungry, we have fresh bagels over there from an honest-to-god Jewish bakery just up the way. You'd swear you were in New York."

76

"Thanks," Marc replied, "but we had a pretty big breakfast at the hotel. I will grab a coffee, though. Dave?"

With a thumbs up from his partner, Marc quickly poured two cups as Sanders continued.

"Since none of us have met, let me go around the table and introduce us. To my right, here, is Tom Sawyer, just like the book. Tom is in charge of operations for our team, which is a nice way of saying he's the guy who gets everything done." Sawyer gave them a little backhanded wave. "Next to him is Peter Nolan, who handles new product development. But he's more of an admin guy, too, and if we decide to work together, he'll be your primary contact at Lockheed for the time being." Peter raised his chin toward them. "Nice to meet you."

Sanders continued. "To my left, respectively, are Evan Clark and Henry Gantt."

"Hank," Henry interjected.

"Right. *Hank*," Sanders acknowledged. "Evan and Hank are our two top guys from Aces Studio, the Microsoft group that was in charge of Flight Simulator before the program was shut down. They came over with a few others when we in-licensed ESP."

"ESP?" Marc wondered. "What's ESP?"

Evan Clark spoke up. "ESP is technically the commercial version of Flight Simulator. Dovetail wound up with the consumer version. There are a few differences between the two, mostly in the area of customizability, and the internal plan back at Aces was to have the two product lines diverge over time so we could sell a higher-margin version to commercial customers like Boeing and the airlines. That was mostly just a way to recapture the higher costs associated with maintaining the business-to-business relationships. When the deal with Lockheed went down, it only made sense for them — *us* — to focus on the ESP product."

"Right, makes perfect sense," Marc agreed. "So what exactly do you two do at Lockheed?"

Hank Gantt jumped in. "Evan and I kind of jointly manage both the development team and the maintenance team. Of course, no one wants to be the guy stuck with maintenance all the time, so splitting up the work between us makes fixing bugs a lot less unpleasant. Plus it keeps us both eyes-on to what's going on with the current version of the code."

"Separate from that, I basically focus on coding and core algorithms," Evan offered, "and Hank is the expert on the various databases that underlie the product."

"The program is really driven by the database," Hank explained. "All of the geographic simulations, all the avatars, and the way the avatars interact with the simulated universe, like whether they can fly or move underwater, their relative speeds and drag coefficients, all of that is stored in the databases. If you want to add a new location or a new kind of airplane or tank or boat, you simply insert some new records into the database, and voilà, there it is."

Dave was right on top of all that. "Yeah, Marc doesn't get down to the code level very much, but from what I've seen so far it's really pretty slick, and the database itself is amazingly efficient given how little code is involved in maintaining it."

"And that's just Version 3," Hank noted with excitement. "Wait 'til you see V4! We've really beefed up the code that manages multiple simultaneous avatars, and we've added some new features that let you blend avatars into clusters, and then break off parts of those clusters at will. That way you can store aircraft on carriers, or model the behavior of a plane that, say, loses part of its horizontal stabilizer—"

"Okay, time for all that later." Sanders redirected the discussion, briefly checking his watch. "Why don't we get into the meat of this meeting to see if we can figure out whether there's a fit between us? I got a good report on you guys from Cal Simmons over at Microsoft. He says his people at the CES show were very impressed with what you folks had accomplished, particularly given the limitations you had regarding access to the core engine and database of Prepar3D. I think his words were along the lines of 'these guys must be f-ing geniuses.' Strong words, coming from a guy at his level. And that's what bought you this meeting today."

Cal Simmons had recently been named the Head of Xbox, reporting to Terry Myerson, executive vice president of the Microsoft's Operating Systems Group. Head of Xbox was in charge of everything even remotely related to the game console, including Microsoft Studios. *No wonder they got back to us so quickly*, Dave thought.

"Well, if either of us is a genius," Marc insisted, "that would be Dave, here. He was a rocket scientist even at Google, which is why I would have never gotten involved in any of this without Dave by my side. I'm just the chief bean counter for the company."

"Not true," countered Dave, who had already flushed scarlet at the compliments. "Marc can handle himself quite well around a block of code, and more than a few times he's helped me out big time when I ran into a mental block on how to make something work. But he has a much better handle on the big picture, the business side of how to make *Dronewars* successful. So, like you and Hank," Dave nodded to Evan, "we try to split up the work so we're playing to each of our individual strengths."

"Okay," interrupted Sanders, "now that the love fest is over, why don't we let you guys walk us through the *Dronewars* program so we can see it for ourselves."

"Sure," Marc agreed. "Where do we plug in—"

Evan moved to help Dave with the laptop, showing him the power outlet and HDMI ports built into the conference table. In seconds Dave was booting up the laptop, it's boot screen projected up on a 70-inch LED display located above the bagels near the door, where everyone had a clear view.

"Before we get into the program itself," Marc began, "it might help to cover a little of the back story for the action.

"*Dronewars* is set in the near distant future, by which I mean the game does not specify an exact date, but you can think of the time frame as more like one to three years out from now, not ten to twenty. So it mirrors a world that is not much different from the one we are facing today.

"In future Earth, the conflict between the followers of radical Islam and Western civilization has reached a fever peak, and the original actions taken by the Western countries to try to keep al-Qaeda and the Islamic State in check have failed, leading to all-out war between the West and radical Islam."

Sanders held up a hand. "Let me stop you there. Isn't this a bit too non-PC, too controversial? I mean, even with everything going on in the Middle East, and even with the terrorist attacks on Paris, San Bernardino and at the Vatican Museum, I don't think you can get away with going on and on about Muslims, particularly putting out a game where you actually shoot and kill them. No matter what horrible things some of them may be doing."

Marc paused, smiling. "Actually, Bob, you not only *can* put out a game that's highly controversial, as it turns out, controversial game play is a big positive. Think *Grand Theft Auto*."

Sanders indicated he didn't catch the reference, so Marc explained. "*Grand Theft Auto* was a video game that emerged in the late '90s. It was a form of simulation that allowed a player to take on the role of a criminal in the fictional town of, at first, Liberty City, which was actually just a stand-in for New York City. In the game, players could steal cars, sell drugs, kill people, and so on. The first version of the game came under withering fire for its 'tremendous violence' in the United States and Europe, and was even banned in Brazil. So did they tone down the game? No! In fact, the publisher for the game had sensationalist stories planted in various tabloid magazines to stir up even more controversy. The game sold like hotcakes.

"By the third version of the game, players could hire prostitutes to get their 'health' back, and then kill the prostitutes to recover the money they had paid them. Women's groups howled, and politically-connected folks like Tipper Gore demanded congressional hearings. But it turns out that there is a very real and very *large* market out there for killing people and abusing women. In a world where you can't get away with doing any of that in real life, a game simulation seemed like the next best thing. Later versions let you have sex with women on-screen, and even record sex tapes of the action. You could drive drunk, torture people, and so on. There was even an expansion pack that featured full frontal nudity. And every time someone screamed about the latest over-the-top atrocity, sales soared even higher. At last count, *GTA* has sold over 200 million copies. *Grand Theft Auto IV*, in the middle of the series, sold $500 million in the first week alone. So, no, I'm not concerned about whether we can convince the great unwashed in America to buy a video game that lets them kill Muslims."

Sanders looked around the table, and everyone was indicating they agreed with Marc's assessment. Evan returned Sanders' unspoken question with a wry smile. "The boy speaks the truth. Wanting to kill terrorists is one of those things that few people will admit to in public, but after what we've seen over the past few years, and after 9-11, I'll admit I get a little thrill every time I hear we've taken one of those bastards off the face of the Earth."

Marc paused for a moment to see if there was any further objection, then shot a quick glance toward his partner. "Dave. Lights! Cameras! Action!"

Dave clicked on the program icon and the demo sprang to life. The screen showed a group of Arabic-looking men in a tan-colored truck driving across a desert landscape. The view was zoomed in on the men in the truck from a perspective that let you see into the truck through the front passenger window, with all four men clearly visible. The men were speaking Arabic.

"How did you get that to work?" asked an astonished Hank. "We can't even do that in Version 4!"

"Well, it did take me a couple of weeks," Dave admitted. "I hacked into the code and inserted a jump instruction in the main loop sequence—"

The view changed to an overhead perspective of the truck driving down a dusty, deserted road, then zoomed out even further and morphed into a cockpit view of what appeared to be an A-10 Warthog strike jet. Dave moved a joystick he was holding to center the truck on crosshairs that had appeared in the middle of the aircraft's windscreen, then pressed a button on the joystick, activating the 30 mm GAU-8 Avenger rotary cannon mounted on the jet. Almost immediately the truck exploded in a hail of depleted uranium armor-piercing shells fired from the cannon.

Sander's eyes were as wide as saucers. "I've flown that A-10 in combat missions, son. That simulation is dead-on accurate."

"Thanks," Dave acknowledged. "Now try this." He tapped another button on the joystick and the view changed to a modest mud-and-wattle house set slightly apart from a group of similar houses. Men dressed in traditional Arab galabayas with automatic rifles slung across their backs were walking in and out of the house. Again, conversations in Arabic could be heard coming from the inside of the building.

"What are they talking about?" Sanders asked.

"Well, not really anything at this point," Dave explained. "I just scammed the audio from a Rosetta Stone disk on learning Arabic. When we get a bit closer to launch we'll have to hire people to record a real sound track." Dave's hands flexed on the controller and the view once again zoomed back. Another button press and the image switched to an angle that resembled a view screen set into some type of computer console. For several moments the view screen was almost completely black, but then a speck of light appeared that quickly resolved into a rapidly swelling image of the house they had seen previously.

"This is the target as seen by the UAV controller. The drone controller. The target is an al-Qaeda in Yemen safe house where the terrorists are planning an attack on the US embassy in Sana'a. The controller has launched a Predator drone strike on the house. I'll switch over to the close-up view of the drone as it zooms in on the house." Dave's fingers danced on the controller, and suddenly the view shifted to a close-in image of the Predator from slightly behind and to the right. Dave moved the joystick to change the camera angle toward the top of the drone and off slightly to the left.

"Whoa, hold on there, cowboy!" Sanders demanded. Dave hit ALT-P on the keyboard in front of him, and the action paused.

Sanders seemed stunned. "I've seen the MQ-1 Predator up front and personal, and what I'm seeing up there on that computer screen looks exactly like the real thing. But DOD has never released any images of the Predator at that level of resolution. How in the hell did you get the pictures to model that so damn perfect?"

Dave gave him a sheepish grin. "Well, not that I'm admitting anything, but my job at Google gave me pretty much unlimited access to their databases, and before I resigned I might have downloaded some content from the databases that would help in making *Dronewars* more realistic—"

"Are you telling me that Google has its hands on classified data from the DOD?" Sanders was beside himself. Who in the hell was responsible for *that* kind of security breach?

"The Google databases have pretty much every secret anyone could ever imagine," Dave answered.

"But what about the privacy laws? I didn't think Google was allowed to do that anymore."

Marc shrugged his shoulders. "In theory, people can opt out of data sharing, either by turning off cookies in their browsers or clicking an opt-out button in various online apps. But the reality is, if you opt out you also lose a great deal of the functionality of services like Google search or Google maps, so very few people actually turn data sharing off. Then there's the issue of so-called zombie or super cookies that automatically store various types of data in Flash Local Stored Objects. A pretty long list of companies have been sued for using supercookie technology. In fact, in 2011, even Microsoft was caught using supercookies on their websites."

Sanders was undeterred. "But the DOD spends a fortune on cybersecurity. There's no way any of this could slip through military firewalls."

"And yet I would challenge you to name a single federal agency or branch of the military that hasn't been hacked at one time or another. And not just by the Chinese or the Russians — by run-of-the-mill hackers acting alone. But Google doesn't need to tunnel through hardened firewalls. Almost any secret the U.S. military thinks it's protecting gets replicated to outside computers owned by contractors and suppliers spread around the world, and a lot of info just walks out the door of military installations on laptops and phones. Remember the case of Ardit Ferizi, who got arrested in Malaysia after he gave ISIS classified information on more than 1,000 U.S. service members, information he hacked from a private company in the United States."

"Just how extensive *is* this Google database? How much top-secret information do they have their hands on?" Sanders asked.

"I'm not sure anyone really knows, because the server capacity has become pretty spread out these days. Nobody wants to lose Google to another big earthquake hitting the Bay Area. But they used to measure Google's data capacity in exabytes, which is ten to the eighteenth power. The last numbers I saw suggested that number may now be in zettabytes, or ten to the twenty-first power. And as to how many secrets are buried in there, there isn't any real way of telling. We're not talking about an active effort to steal information, it's all just automatic data collection. What you had for breakfast, who you're sleeping around with, the game score from last night you Googled. It's all in there — nothing really gets deleted on the Internet."

"Okay. Good to know, I guess." Sanders, obviously flustered, motioned for Dave to continue.

On screen, the Predator was rapidly closing in on its target. "As we know, the Predator is a drone, not a missile, so it doesn't actually impact a target. Instead, the drone is equipped with two AGM-114 Hellfire missiles, or, depending upon the mission, sometimes some other kind of weapons. Now, once the Predator has locked on to its target, and while it is still a safe distance away, the drone operator in the remote ground control station fires the missiles—" A flash of flame, and two Hellfires were suddenly streaking toward the house. "A Hellfire missile is roughly five feet long and seven inches in diameter. Its operational range is around five miles, at a top speed of Mach 1.3, or a little less than a thousand miles per hour." The missiles struck the house dead center, lighting up the screen with the simulated explosion. The sound of the explosion was impressive, even given the monitor's small speakers. "There are several different types of warheads available for the

Hellfire. Here I used an eighteen-pound shaped charge. More than enough to do the job." The smoke cleared, revealing that very little was left of the former one-story house. The Predator swooped over the blast site, its camera angling down and zooming in to show the resulting debris and carnage in gory detail.

Sanders let out a low whistle. "I can see why the guys at Microsoft were so impressed. And you did all this with just our developer kit?" he asked.

"Well, it took quite a bit of hacking into the code for a lot of this. I sort of built a wrapper around the Prepar3D code, and I used some of the sim stuff I had built at Google to improve the realism and insert some of the extra control screens. If I had to, I could build the entire game that way, but I would much rather do it the easy way, just fleshing out the source code. Plus, we have the matter of porting all this over to the Xbox."

"Damn. I thought *I* was good—" Evan looked over at Dave and Marc with a new-found respect. "We don't even have anything running in Version Four that's at this level of sophistication. I am *really* going to look forward to working with you guys!"

"Let's not get ahead of ourselves," cautioned Sanders, but it was obvious from the quick glances around the table that Dave's demo had won them all over. "So it's clear you guys have the technical chops to pull this off. Question is, do you have the right people and resources? And as impressive as this is, it doesn't mean doodly if the game ain't right, if the players don't find the action compelling."

"You're spot on, Bob," Marc agreed. "And to be honest, neither Dave nor I are really the right people to drive the game play. Just like every other red-blooded American boy, we both had our own Xboxes and Playstations at various times growing up, but neither of us were what you would call serious gamers. We didn't get to where we were at Google by wasting our time playing games. But we know a lot of people who are, and Austin is just dripping with serious gamers. So I've been slowly recruiting a kind of combo focus group/alpha tester team to give us continuing feedback on what they want to see in the game. Plus, I've put together an analysis of the games that really took off, and what features seem to drive them. I'd be happy to share that with you guys if you want."

"That would be great. I think Evan and Hank would love to take a gander at that." Sanders checked the two guys from Aces, who were silently agreeing. "In the meantime, why don't you tell us about how you see the game working from the user's point of view."

Marc nodded. "To begin with, even though *Dronewars* is built on top of a simulation engine, that doesn't drive the game play very much. The sim is just there to provide a high level of realism, and to allow us to spread the action out across the planet in various locations, while still maintaining the realism of those locations. Realism has always been the Holy Grail of gaming, and the more texture we can add, the better the total immersion experience for the players."

Marc continued, pointing back at the monitor. "And even though the game has some strong elements of firing weapons from a first person perspective, it isn't exactly a first person shooter, either. What we're trying to accomplish is some mishmash of first person, strategy, sim and MMO, with a few other approaches sprinkled in here and there as well. That's one reason we think it will be so compelling — it offers a wide variety of gaming experiences simultaneously."

He arched an eye toward Evan and Hank for confirmation. With all their experience at Aces, they were probably the best equipped people in the room to follow what he was talking about. Evan was the first to speak up. "I like it. That's always been a big problems with these games. No matter how good the game action is, at some point the boredom factor kicks in. You can only blast so many zombies or aliens with so many different kinds of virtual weapons before it all starts to be a case of been there, done that."

"Exactly," Marc agreed. "So we try to mix it all up, add extra layers of complexity that keeps the players engaged, keeps them constantly exploring new ways to do things. And the other thing we're adding in here is the randomness of the opponent. Almost all conventional games feature opponents driven by computer algorithms. That is important, because it lets you play the game by yourself when no one else is around. But, increasingly, players are turning to online gaming where the other side is an avatar driven by another human being. That makes the game play much less predictable, and it has the added bonus of making beating the other guy so much more satisfying. You didn't just beat the game, the computer, you beat down another person. If you're twenty years old, unemployed and living at home, and playing the game late at night in your parents' basement with a bag of Cheetos at your feet, that's a game changer. No pun intended."

Sanders interjected. "But I thought this game was about fighting terrorists. How in the world will you get people to take on the side of the terrorists?"

"Don't worry. There will always be people who prefer the Dark Side of the Force," Marc replied in his best Lord Vader rumble.

Hank held up a finger, raising another point. "But if I'm on the side of ISIS, or particularly al-Qaeda, then most of the action will be about blowing myself up with a suicide vest. Other than getting maybe a great end-of-action sequence of going to paradise and nailing some virgins, that sounds pretty quick and brutal. Not a whole lot of fun for the guy playing the terrorist."

Marc agreed with Hank's point. "And that's why I said this isn't really a first person shooter — that's where the strategy portion kicks in. It's the same problem from the other side, as well. If all you've got is one Predator and two Hellfire missiles, once you've shot your load you're out of the action. But in *Dronewars* you're going to have lots of different targets, and lots of different weapons. A suicide bomber is just one of those weapons. And, we haven't exactly worked out all the details yet, but as you succeed and manage to avoid being fatally damaged, you'll get replenished, you'll get more weapons and harder targets. So the better you get at the game, the longer your gaming session lasts. And perhaps there will be some kind of points system or a promotion to some harder level.

All that is pretty commonplace in these kinds of video games, but we'll need some good feedback from our testers to nail down exactly how that will work."

"Not being a gamer myself," Sanders pointed out, "you boys have lost me a bit with all that. But I want to shift this discussion over to some of the other issues, and in particular what you might need from us, and what Lockheed can get out the relationship." Sanders paused and settled back a bit in his seat. "First of all, as you've already pointed out, getting your hands on the source code for Prepar3D will be key for you guys. I would think you could also benefit greatly from spending some time with our development guys." Sanders hooked his thumb in Evan and Hank's direction. "And from what they've said, that might actually go both ways.

"Second, you need to get certified by Microsoft for the Xbox developer program. I think we can make that happen toot sweet, assuming we all decide to go forward with this. Lockheed can rubberstamp your application, and Cal Simmons indicated that would be all they would need to get everything Fedexed to you by the end of the week. I think Evan has some folks who already know their way around the Xbox code, and I believe Evan himself worked some on the Xbox port of Flight Simulator at Aces before Microsoft shut the group down, so I can spare him a bit to help get you guys up and running."

"I still have a lot of code from the port," Evan offered. "It's changed a bit for Xbox One and its various follow-ons, and there are

92

a few other changes you'd need to dive into for the next gen Xbox, but it would get you most of the way there."

"That would be super. Thanks!" Dave could already see many of his coding headaches melting away.

"Third," Sanders continued, "is the question of money. I understand you guys are footing the bill out of your own pockets."

"Between salaries, bonuses and stock options at Google, Dave and I were able to sock away a lot of money," Marc noted.

"Yeah, well there's money, and then there's *money*." Sanders leaned forward suggestively. "The first mistake to make in any new business is to go in underfunded. You wind up cutting corners, and in the end it all blows up in your face. You fail. We've already talked about some of the corners you guys have been cutting, and you're just getting started. Keep this up, and you're going to crash and burn, for sure."

Sanders wagged a finger at Marc. "Thing is, I don't want to be associated with failure. As they say at NASA, failure is not an option. If we go forward with this, then, I have some discretionary items in the budget and some other things I can move around to help you guys out, starting with giving you some time from my people." He nodded again toward Evan and Hank, who were sitting impassively, taking it all in. "But if I do that, if Lockheed agrees to help you guys get this game put together and get it launched, then Lockheed is going to need a few things in return."

Marc looked over at his partner, fighting to keep his thoughts from showing on his face. "Sure, we're open. What do you suggest?"

"First, let me give you boys some background. You probably walked in here thinking that Prepar3D was just a training simulator, a tool to let new soldiers and pilots get up to speed on their various weapons and equipment. And to some degree, you'd be right.

"But our mission is morphing. The brass in Washington have decided to expand the simulations to include large-scale war gaming exercises."

Evan and Hank looked stunned, like this was the first time they had ever heard anything about this.

"War games are big business for the DOD," Sanders continued." Part of the point of war games is to improve operational readiness of our armed forces, and to practice coordination of various maneuvers both within our own armed forces as well as with our partners from other countries. War games are also useful to send a signal to hostile countries that the United States is ready, willing and able to strike with deadly force in any and every corner of this godforsaken planet.

"But the downside is, war games are very expensive. And they are also very dangerous, because the difference between a game and actual combat is a very thin line. Finally, and this is very important, just like flight training where you can simulate a dangerous malfunction or some other unexpected complication, DOD is interested in simulating war games scenarios that might be too dangerous or complicated to actually test in real life. Or scenarios that we would rather not share with those hostile countries

94

I mentioned. And they want to do a *lot* of those scenarios, which would be cost prohibitive if we conducted live fire exercises.

"So the net is, I've been tasked with scaling up Prepar3D to support these mega-scale virtual war games. The problem is, I don't have near enough resources at this point, and the resources I do have don't have near enough expertise to make that happen. No insult intended," he added, indicating Evan and Hank.

"None taken, sir," Hank responded. "I think what we just saw in the demo makes that point pretty clear."

"Right," Sanders continued, turning to Marc and Dave. "And so, that's where you guys come in. I already had a chat with Cal at Microsoft to be on the lookout for someone with the talent to pull this off, and after your demo at CES he shot me an email suggesting I take a gander. And I really like what I saw, at least what I've seen so far. There's still a lot of work to be done, but from where I sit this looks like a potential win-win for both of us, about an eighty or ninety percent overlap between what you need for your game and what we need for the war games sims."

"Ok-a-a-ay," Marc drawled, still apparently struggling to make sense out of what he'd just heard. "At this point, I don't see any red flags to speak of. As far as working on a DOD project, I personally don't have any ethical problems with that. And Dave, here," he said, motioning toward his partner, "comes from a military background. His dad was Air Force, and I think his grandfather served in Korea, so no pushback there." Dave agreed. "But... so far all we've talked about is an Islamic warfare model. Surely you're going to need something on a much larger scale than that."

"In the end, yes, we're going to need something much, much larger. Certainly, for the U.S. military, fighting radical Islam is one component. But our biggest war games effort would be targeted toward Putin and China. For Russia, we've got the Ukraine and all of its fallout, so we've got to model stopping Russian aggression on its western and southern borders, as well as in the contested waters off northern Canada. That's a red hot topic right now, unless we want to wake up and find ourselves facing a new and improved version of the old Soviet empire.

"In addition, Russian subs and warships have increasingly been positioning themselves along the path of the undersea communications cables between North America and Europe. Although there are robots in place down there to repair any minor breaches in the cables, a major disruption of communications traffic through the cables would most likely devastate Western economies.

"As for China, the Reds have been building up their armed forces at a furious pace over the last few decades, largely taking advantage of weapons designs they've pilfered from our own military and our contractors. More recently, China has been constructing new islands in the South China Sea near the Spratly Islands, dumping sediment dredged up from the ocean floor onto existing reefs, and then topping them with airfields, port facilities and other military buildings. Their ultimate aim is to claim ownership and control over that part of the world, which includes highly strategic sea lanes and a vast fortune in undersea oil and gas reserves. Our Navy has been conducting ongoing exercises in the region to send a strong message that China needs to back off, but DOD would dearly love to explore other options, particularly if the Chinese decide to flex their military muscles to back up their claims."

"And little two-man Rocketship is the answer to all this?" Marc asked incredulously.

Sanders chuckled. "As they say, it's not the size of the dog in the fight, it's the size of the fight in the dog. You're right, by yourself you would have zero chance of pulling this off. Heck, all by yourself I think you have pretty much zero chance of even getting a game out the door. But you have the right ideas, the right talent. And you guys are *hungry*. I'll take a hungry dog over a fat and lazy dog any day of the week."

Marc still wasn't convinced. "But the *scale* of what you're proposing—"

Sanders shook his head. "Scale isn't a problem. Lockheed has scale. The DOD has scale in spades, if we can just get this to the point where they have confidence we can deliver. And one last thing—" Sanders prepared to drop his trump card. "We have access to databases Google could only dream about. Geo databases of the entire planet with satellite imagery accurate to about a one-inch resolution, with real-time updates. Computer-aided design models of every weapon in the U.S. arsenal, and similar models for all of the hostile arsenals. Name any weapon, any aircraft, any naval warship, and I can have a working virtual model to you in less than a day. Pop that into your Xbox One and smoke it."

Dave was blown away by the idea, and glancing quickly over at Marc, he could see his partner's gears beginning to spin at full speed. This could be HUGE! He turned back toward the head of the table, where Sanders had the hungry look of a cat about to pounce. *He has us,* Dave thought, *and he knows it.* And that wasn't necessarily a bad thing.

19

The meeting broke up soon afterwards, with Sanders promising them a nondisclosure agreement from legal by the end of the week. As soon as that was signed, he'd get the source code out to them and get the Xbox application expedited at Microsoft. A limo was waiting to take them to the airport, but their flight wasn't until later in the afternoon, so Evan suggested the four of them could grab lunch nearby. He would get them to the airport afterwards.

They spent lunch comparing notes, and Hank — who had been at Microsoft for almost ten years before he was finally canned — regaled them with tales of the various misdeeds and mishaps he had experienced at the company. Perhaps his funniest story was the launch of Microsoft Bob in 1995, several years before Hank joined the company. Microsoft Bob was an attempt to put a more user-friendly face on Microsoft Windows, and worked as an overlay to Windows that hid the details of the operating system from the user. Instead of the Windows desktop, a user booting up a PC with Bob installed would see a cartoon version of a desktop sitting in a virtual living room, with a cartoon dog trotting in to offer help and various tips. To start a program, you would click on a stylized object in the room representing that program. For example, clicking on some sheets of paper lying on the desktop would start Letter Writer, an extremely simplistic word processor. Hank explained that Microsoft Bob wound up being more appropriate for children than for grown adults, although even a child would quickly grow tired of its sluggish, tedious interface and the equally insipid but ever-present dog. Bob was one of the first consumer products that Bill Gates personally had a hand in launching, and it quickly became one of the biggest and most glaring failures in Microsoft history. Both Microsoft insiders and outsiders with pre-launch access to the program advised the company to bury the product before launch. In fact, outsiders didn't just dislike Bob, they actually seemed angry that it had even been developed. But the real secret to the product's development and launch, and Bill Gates' personal involvement in all of it, lay in the fact that the marketing manager for Bob was none other than Melinda French. Bill Gates' girlfriend, soon to become Melinda Gates. Hank got a real kick out of that. "Well, at least Bill got a wife out of the deal!"

And for Dave, the moral of Microsoft Bob was unmistakable: Don't let your commitment to a particular idea blind you as to whether or not it makes sense to your target market.

As lunch broke up, the four of them exchanged contact info, and Evan took Marc and Dave back to the Hyatt. Bidding them goodbye, Evan promised to get the source code and the Xbox port code out to Dave as soon as the nondisclosure was inked, and Dave promised to shoot Evan a copy of the wrapper code he had built around Prepar3D in return.

On the flight back to Austin, Marc and Dave were still pretty geared up about the meeting.

"One thing I still don't get," Dave wondered. "Why do they care about our getting involved in Xbox development? Seems like that would take some focus away from finishing the core code for the war gaming engine."

"I asked Sanders about that while you were in the bathroom. It seems they have the same concerns we have about hosting the program on a PC. Too many hardware and software variables to deal with, and the cost of specing a PC that could handle all the horsepower requirements for the program would be prohibitive. Targeting a single game console solves all that."

"Well, it does if we assume that the console is Xbox Ultimate, and that the new console solves all the problems with the graphics processor Evan was describing over lunch. It doesn't sound like the Xbox One can keep up with everything we're planning on throwing at it."

"Yeah," Marc agreed. "Maxing out at 30 frames per second just to get it to 1080p, much less 4k, I think that might be a bitch to work around. And even One X struggles with that."

"It's not that I can't do it." Dave was confident that he could pull off almost any miracle when it came to code. "It's just going to affect the richness of what I can put on-screen at any moment, so users will have to switch view modes more often. And unless we can crank it up to 45 frames a second per eye, we'll never be able to pull off 3D at anything higher than 720p without causing major headaches. And I mean *real* headaches. Ideally I would like to see 4K and true 60 fps per eye. We could do some real magic with that."

"I agree, but it's not really up to us. We'll have to see what Microsoft comes up with down the road, and what they're ultimately able to launch with. And we're still going to have to build in backwards compatibility for the original Xbox One and maybe even the 360, or we won't get the volume we need at launch. So we sex it up for 4k, but we keep 1080 or even 720 as a fallback option either way."

"Yeah, makes sense," Dave agreed. "But I don't want to seem like I'm bitching. Today went very well. Actually, it went amazingly well. If even half of what we talked about today comes true, you and I are *golden*, bro."

"I'll take seventy-five percent, but I'm with you, Dave. Things are finally starting to go our way."

Just then the flight attendants wheeled up with the drink cart. Marc ordered a rum and Diet Coke for both of them, and they toasted the first break they had seen in a very long time. Rocketship finally seemed to be on its way to the stars.

shock the world

20

The nondisclosure arrived in Marc's email the very next day. After a quick check-in with their lawyer, it was signed, scanned and on its way back to Lockheed.

Almost immediately, Dave's phone pinged with a new message. "Hey, Evan sent over the code!" Dave rushed over to the development computer, pulling up his email and downloading the code. Just a few seconds later, thanks to his high-speed Google fiber Internet connection, the download was complete and Dave was quickly flipping through the Prepar3D source code, then through the code for the Xbox port.

"Awesome! It's all C++!" The code was all written in object-oriented C++, a language Dave knew by heart — possibly even better than his English. Historically, most modern game designers preferred to code in C++, a computer language that allows for high-level abstraction while also giving programmers low-level control whenever speed or precision is critical. In contrast, Microsoft had recently been trying to woo Xbox programmers over to C#, which despite its name has little in common with C++. In particular, where C++ gives programmers complete control over the allocation and placement of objects in memory, C# relegates memory management to the overarching .Net framework. And that all translated into bloated programs and sluggish game play. Dave regarded C# programmers as amateurs, which was probably somewhat unfair, but given the limitations of the Xbox hardware he was glad to see that the code was in a format that would allow him to squeeze every last ounce of speed out of the console.

Marc, of course, couldn't care less about any of this, other than the fact that Dave seemed to be in his element. Whatever kept Dave happy and fully productive was okay by him. "It's getting pretty late in the day, buddy, and you know we promised to take the girls to a movie at the Alamo. Don't get yourself so buried in all that code that you can't crawl out." The Alamo Drafthouse Cinema is a hybrid restaurant/movie theater that had sprung up in north central Austin in the late 1990's.

"Yeah, you're right, this can wait 'til tomorrow," Dave agreed reluctantly. "But I'm really excited about the code for the port. It looks like it's pretty close to finished, other than making some changes in the DirectX calls and cleaning up some of the memory management. Of course I'll know better when we get our hands on the Xbox SDK—"

"Working on it." Marc grabbed a Diet Coke and plopped down on the couch. "Sanders says he already touched base with Cal at Microsoft, and after we shuffle some paperwork back and forth, we should get it by the end of next week."

"Okay, I'll hold off worrying about the port until later. I've got a lot of work to do, anyway, just getting up to speed on all the mods they made for Prepar3D."

"Timing wise, when do you think would be a good time to swing back out to Orlando to go over all that with Evan and Hank's people? If we can get at least a two-week window, the tickets will be a whole lot cheaper." Marc was pulling up Expedia on his tablet, and cross-checking the flights with Southwest. "Looks like I can get you a round-trip on Southwest for about three hundred, and there are a bunch of suite hotels clustered around Lockheed. Good time to be going out there, too, because it's still a bit chilly for Disney and Universal, and the older kids are all in school, so the prices aren't too bad."

"That'll work for me," Dave answered. "In the meantime, if anything big pops up we can always Skype. But at some point I could really use their help identifying all the code changes that we'll need to port over, and working through the various database hooks. And I'm pretty much going to have to abandon most of what we did for the demo. Now that we can make the changes directly to the code, those hacks don't really help, and I don't think they would work on Xbox anyway."

"Makes sense," Marc replied, giving him a thumbs up. "It's probably going to be a while before we need another demo, anyway. Time to dump that stuff out on the highway and get on down the road. And along those lines, before we get much further down that road, we need to sketch out all the changes we agreed to yesterday, and how all of that is going to affect the look and feel of the game."

"I agree, and I've already made some notes on that, Marc. Let's block off tomorrow and maybe Saturday if we need to, while everything is still fresh in our minds. And I'll set up a conference call with the guys in Orlando for maybe Monday, if that works, to cover the questions I know are going to pop up."

"Good plan," Marc agreed, checking his watch. "Look, I need to pour over the draft of the interim partnership agreement Sanders sent over, but why don't we plan to break out of here around 5:30. Even with traffic that'll give us plenty of time to change and pick up the ladies. I got tickets online for the Alamo on South Lamar, so we're set."

"Great. I've got to pick up Jules at the shop, so why don't we meet there and go together? We can grab a bottle from the back of the store and have a glass of wine before the movie."

"Like the way you think, buddy," Marc turned to the forty-page draft agreement on his tablet. It was pretty impressive how fast the legal staff at Lockheed had turned this around, but Dave had voiced a sneaky suspicion that the paperwork had all been completed well in advance, and the lawyers just used find and replace to fill in the blanks. *Not that it matters much*, Marc thought. *The agreement is just a formality. The key is, now we've just got to deliver.*

21

Dave dragged in a little late the next morning, his head still pounding from the night before. Marc was already hard at work at the electronic whiteboard, sketching out an outline of all the proposed changes. A tall stack of papers on one corner of the desk suggested this wasn't his first whiteboard full of notes.

"Good morning, Sleeping Beauty!" Marc greeted, a little too cheerfully for Dave's throbbing head.

"Sleeping ugly is more like it," Dave replied. "I don't get it. You had *way* more to drink last night than I did, and yet here you are, showing no signs of any of it. How do you do it?"

"Practice, my man. They don't let you into marketing unless you can prove you have the alcoholic *cojones* to hold your own. And, by the way, I take it your night went as well as mine when you got home?"

The girls had spent part of their Tuesday night alone together shopping at Tabu, a lingerie store in north Austin. After getting home from the movie they each had a surprise in store for their respective boyfriends.

"Oh, yeah," Dave grinned. "Hard to believe, though, that so little could cost so much, especially since it spends so little time on."

"I guess it's kind of like the line, Why are divorces so expensive?" Marc noted. "Because they're worth it."

"Well, definitely worth whatever Jules spent on it."

"Yeah, I told Elle, if this is what I have to look forward to every time I go out of town, maybe I should leave more often. Correction: I told her that this morning, not last night." Marc chuckled. "Timing is everything."

"You got that right," Dave agreed. "So what you got up here?" he asked, motioning toward the list Marc had drawn up on the board.

"Just thought I'd get a head start while you were sleeping it off. Let me flip back to the first page—" Marc picked up the remote for the electronic whiteboard and pulled up the first screen he had saved to memory.

"My idea is to start with some of the big picture items, then move on to more and more of the details." Dave seemed to be in agreement, so Marc continued. "The first issue is the code bifurcation, which actually happens on multiple levels. According to the deal with Lockheed, we have two programs in the hopper, not just one. The first program, of course, is *Dronewars*, and the second is the specialized war gaming software. For lack of a better name, I thought we might use the codename *Warg* for that."

Dave laughed at that. "I like it! That works on so many levels."

"I thought you would. Nice and short, a contraction for war games, the whole notion of entering another animal or object and controlling it from afar. You don't think it's a little too *stark*, though, do you?" Marc asked.

"OUCH! Show some mercy for my aching head!" Dave made a big show of grabbing his head in response to Marc's pun.

"Well, show up on time and maybe I won't have so much time on my hands to think up these things." Marc laughed, turning back to the board. "Okay, seriously. My thought is that we ignore this bifurcation for now. We really don't have any idea of what the differences are going to look like in the end, so worrying about it right now gets us nowhere."

Dave agreed.

"Similarly," Marc continued, "based on what we learned from our lunch with the Aces guys, Microsoft is planning to launch Xbox Ultimate sometime this summer. One of the key features of Ultimate is a dedicated multicore GPU that theoretically solves the problem of the currently underpowered graphics processor unit. Where we would be lucky to see 1080p at 30 frames per second on Xbox One — and a little better for One X, no matter what kind of magic dust you throw at it — Ultimate will supposedly support 4k resolution at 120 fps, or 60 fps if we split it for 3D."

"But," Dave interrupted, "at this point we can't really count on that. First of all, Microsoft has a notoriously bad track record delivering on their promises. Remember that story Hank told us about Winpad. They left a lot of very important people hanging out to dry on that one, and wiped out a bunch of small companies who had bet their lunch on the Winpad launch."

Winpad was a small hand-held computer that Microsoft had developed in the early 1990's, lining up a long list of hardware and software partners, both big and small, to support a fall 1994 launch. The project was super-secret at the time, with third party partners agreeing to never even mention the name Winpad in public, even though Microsoft comically capped a private 1993 developer's conference for the product by handing out dozens of Winpad hats, bags and pens. But Apple beat Microsoft to the punch with the 1993 launch of its own personal digital assistant, the Newton. Newton launched with great fanfare and expectations, but the praise quickly turned to ridicule, largely due to Newton's horrendously inaccurate handwriting recognition. Even though it was quickly becoming clear that Newton had poisoned the well for handheld devices, Microsoft continued to march feverishly toward launch, demanding that the small companies who had signed on as Winpad partners have their programs completed in time for launch. Just weeks before the scheduled launch, though, Microsoft suddenly pulled the plug on the device, leaving all of those companies to swallow the huge development costs for software they would never get a chance to sell.

"Right, we'll need to keep a sharp eye on that," Marc agreed. "Plus, we still have to worry about backwards-compatibility for Xbox One, in addition to One X and Ultimate buyers who don't spring for the 4k television sets right up front. Which means that while we might add 4k features at some point, the program design can't rely exclusively on 4k."

"I'd agree with that plan," Dave offered. "Let's stay focused on what we can wring out of the current box, and worry about

112

scaling it up for a possible 4k down the road a bit when things get a little clearer."

Marc turned back to the board and underlined the word Summer. "While we're on the subject of Ultimate, though, and this is a bit off topic, do you think we can be ready with *Dronewars* in time for a summer launch in concert with Ultimate?"

Dave took a moment to think about that. "I don't know. I think part of that answer depends upon where in summer we're talking — early, middle or late. My guess, based upon history, is that they'll want to launch it more toward September, to take advantage of some of the game conferences going on about then, and to get the buzz going full steam for the Christmas selling season. Plus, when did Microsoft ever make a launch deadline? If they're saying summer now, they'll be chopping features well into August to get it out the door."

"Okay, Dave, so let's say August/September. Is it doable?"

Dave walked over to stare out the window, deep in thought, mentally walking week by week through the development cycle. "I think we'll have a better grip on that in two or three weeks, after I get a chance to get my hands on the code and see just how big of a challenge we're facing. But if I can get some help from Lockheed on avatar development, and the Aces guys can help out a bit with the work on the game control servers, I think it could be done. That's assuming, of course," Dave cautioned, mimicking an explosion with his hands, "nothing blows up on us along the way."

"I'll take that as a firm maybe." Marc put a check next to Summer on the board. "Next. We need to revisit the back story for the game. Assuming we add in the Russian/Chinese component, which is still a big if, how do we fold that into the Middle East War scenario?"

"I've got some ideas on that, Marc, that are kind of in opposition to each other. Can I get a new screen on that thing?" Marc saved the current page, then hit New Page on the remote. Dave walked over to the board and wrote PRO on one side and CON on the other. "First of all, on the con side, just because we agreed to a Russian/Chinese component for *Warg*," Dave explained, already adopting their new codename for the war games version of the program, "doesn't mean we need to include it in *Dronewars*." He wrote the word 'bifurcate' under CON.

"But won't that mean extra work for us?" Marc asked.

"No, it really isn't any extra work at all, at least from the perspective of the overall two-version project. It's just a matter of not turning on that functionality in *Dronewars*, but leaving it in place for *Warg*."

"Gotcha," Marc answered, "but that means we wind up doing a lot of work for Lockheed that we don't get to take advantage of for the game."

"Exactly," Dave noted. "So on the pro side, figuring out how to tie the Russians and Chinese into the game play makes a lot of sense in terms of making *Dronewars* more playable." Dave wrote 'better game' under PRO.

114

"But stick with me, here, Marc," Dave continued, " 'cause I'm about to throw a monkey wrench into all this." He walked over to sit on the edge of the desk, using the electronic marker in his hand for emphasis. "Up to this point I've been mostly focused on getting the demo to work for your dog and pony show, and all of that is from the perspective of the good guys, the Americans. But in the back of my head I've been struggling with how this would look from the point of view of the terrorists. As you recall, Sanders brought up that issue in Orlando."

"He wondered who would want to take the side of the terrorists," Marc said, still trying to figure out where Dave was going with all this.

"Right. But that's not the real problem, here," Dave agreed, shaking his head. "The bigger issue is, with the exception of limited battlefield engagements with ISIS, the biggest weapons the terrorists have, and the weapons that account for almost all of their attacks on the West, are car bombs and suicide vests. With me so far?"

"Yeah, go on."

"So we answered the question of how to deal with continuing game play after your avatar terrorist blows himself up, by simply giving him a lot of suicide bombers to work with. But every time I dig into the problem of how to graphically represent those attacks in the game, taken from the point of view of the terrorist, I get the same ugly answer. *Grand Theft Auto* aside, graphically portraying someone walking into a crowd of innocent people and blowing himself up, blowing all of them up at the same time, it just doesn't work. And think about the Predator fly-by in the demo, where we swoop down on all the mangled bodies. After the bomb goes off, what do we show then? The mangled corpses of innocent little children? This isn't a matter of beating up a prostitute, or killing another crime boss, all in a cartoon-style resolution. We're talking about something that is actually *sickening*, and all of it in 4k resolution. Even if you could find someone who got off on that kind of action, I don't think I could live with myself if I was responsible for making that happen, for programming that into the game. I discussed all this with Elle the other day, and she agreed. It's a real problem for us."

"I hear you, Dave, but what are you proposing?" Marc understood what Dave was saying, but it was just so *late* in the project to be thinking about this.

"I just don't think we thought it all through before now, Marc. I think we were looking at this at an abstract level, but it didn't start becoming real to me until I completed those Predator scenes, and until I started trying to figure out how to demo the terrorist side. So what I'm saying is, maybe this Lockheed deal was a real blessing in ways we never considered before now."

"So you're saying we should drop the Middle East component entirely and just focus on the Russians and Chinese?" All of this was so new, and Marc seemed to be struggling to work through all the nuances.

"Well, we can leave in the ISIS part, and even the roadside bombing and military aspects of the car bombing, but handle all that

116

more as weapons, like the drones. And I think we should pull back a bit on the realism of the post-action gore, on both sides. Leave in the *suggestion* of blown up bodies without actually showing all the body parts lying around."

"Okay," Marc responded. "Obviously you've been thinking about this a while, and I'm just catching up, so give me a little time to think it all through. But my gut tells me you're right. Why don't we table this for now, and move on to other issues." Marc saw a brief hint of concern flash across Dave's face. "No, I'm with you on this, Dave. Don't worry. It's just that it changes my whole mental picture of the game, how to position it from a marketing perspective, and I need some time to sort all that out. Let's pick it back up this afternoon, okay?"

"Works for me," Dave agreed, tossing Marc the electronic marker. "So what's next?"

They spent the rest of the day working through the details of their new partnership with Lockheed. By late afternoon they had agreed on a new back story involving war against a joint Russian-Chinese alliance, with simultaneous conflicts involving North Korea and the Middle East. Following Sander's suggestions, they penciled in possible airstrikes against Iranian nuclear facilities, but thought that might be better suited for *Warg* than for *Dronewars*.

Dave was eager to dive into the Prepar3D source code, and Elle wanted Marc to join her for a romantic weekend touring the wineries in Fredericksburg, out west of Austin in the Texas Hill

Country, so they decided to blow off meeting again until after the weekend.

Dave picked up his phone and called Julia to check on her plans for the evening, and she reminded him *again* that she had a wine and cheese party planned for the shop after closing to show off a new line of jewelry she was launching, *Jules' Jewels*. With Julia tied up for the night, Dave decided to take advantage of the extra free time to see if he could get the Prepar3D source code to compile. When Marc left him, Dave was already deep into compiler switches and chasing down lines of code that kept popping up as errors. Marc thoughtfully set a timer on Dave's phone before he left, and three hours later Dave's smartwatch buzzed, alerting him to the fact that it was nine o'clock. He reluctantly packed it all in and headed home, frustrated that he couldn't get the program to compile. He had scheduled a video call with the Aces guys for Monday morning to discuss the code, and the alpha dog in him chafed at the idea of having to ask them for help.

22

By the time the Monday morning Skype call rolled around, Dave had made a great deal more progress with the code. Not only was the flight simulator from Lockheed compiling, but he was also able to splice in some of the features from the original demo, and was finally getting a handle on where all of the key functionality was located in the code. It was now all too clear to him that Lockheed's software had been written by teams of programmers and then hacked by other programmers later on to add new features, because the code lacked the elegance and organization that were Dave's signature.

And the code was *loose*. In the old days, when disk storage and memory were tight and computer chips sluggish, programmers prided themselves on writing tight, efficient code to wring the most out of limited resources. But modern computers had become bloated, with ever faster processors and seemingly endless increases in memory and storage. In 1965, Intel co-founder Gordon Moore predicted that transistor density in integrated circuits, the primary factor driving increasing processor speed, would double every two years. It was an eerily accurate observation that quickly gained the title "Gordon's Law." Even modern smart phones contained hundreds of thousands of times more memory than the original IBM PC. And as computers became faster and disk storage exploded, programmers got sloppier and sloppier, especially when they worked in teams, with each sub team focusing on just tiny pieces of the overall program. Program code came to resemble quilts more than blankets, with the different programming and documentation styles of the various sub teams glaringly evident in the code. Even worse, since Team A knew next to nothing about Team B's code, other than the generic interface they were given to activate it, the modular nature of the code translated into sluggishness and inefficiency.

That was the state of the Prepar3D source code as Dave dove into it Saturday morning. By late Saturday he had identified at least twenty five percent of the code that didn't seem to do anything at all, just vestigial code remnants left behind by programmers too lazy to delete it, or afraid to delete it because they didn't know whether or not another team's code was still using it. Tracking down all of the abandoned code took time, but it was critically important, the programming equivalent of clearing out scruffy cedar trees and brush so you could see the majestic old oak trees beyond.

In the process, Dave began to reorganize the code, putting similar components into individual files with clearly explanatory names, like combining all of the string functions into a file called strings.cpp. He also made separate copies of each of the code modules, using the copies to mark up code that he could tell at a glance needed to either be tightened up or reworked entirely.

Before the conference call, Dave packed all of these changes into a compressed tar file that he emailed to Evan and Hank. He made a mental note to set up a joint cloud folder for sharing in the future, where he could park the Visual SourceSafe database for the project. That way they wouldn't have to keep track of emailed versions of the code, and any changes would be automatically replicated to multiple computers for backup. The last thing Dave needed was for a disk crash or a break-in to wipe out months of hard work on the project.

The conference call went smoothly. Dave was careful not to offend the Aces team when he discussed the changes he had already made to the code. To their credit, they acknowledged they already knew it was a problem, but one they couldn't get permission from higher-ups to fix. Evan helped Dave identify some of the function calls and procedure calls that had morphed so much over the years that their original name no longer accurately reflected their use, and in the middle of the discussion Hank realized that he had forgotten to send over an electronic guidebook to the Prepar3D database, a guidebook that would be critical to understanding where and how various objects in the program were stored.

An unexpected new party to the call was Carla Walburg, a recent Lockheed hire. Carla was the group's expert on back end control servers, the centralized servers that fed real-time data on weather conditions and air traffic control to the flight simulation software, and coordinated simultaneous simulations, allowing multiple users to interact with one another. If, for example, several users wanted to simulate a flight in formation, the control server fed each user the relative position, speed and attitude of all the other simulated planes in the formation. Sanders hadn't included Carla in the original meeting because he didn't think she had much to contribute at that stage, but now that the project had been green lighted, Carla was given full responsibility to work with Dave on the back end server requirements.

Carla had a low, husky voice, with just a hint of her native German roots. Her hair was decidedly un-German, black as night and cut very short. She had a no-nonsense way of speaking, with just a hint of mischief. Dave decided he liked her right away.

"Right now, your copy of the software will interact natively with our main servers, but we're going to need to change that pretty quickly," Carla was saying. "I've got an idle server here that we can repurpose to use as a back end for *Warg*. Kind of underpowered, but way more than enough for what you'll need for testing until we get much closer to launch." The Lockheed team had already picked up on and approved of the codename for their version of the program. Carla suggested they might even want to swap names with *Dronewars*, but Dave didn't think Marc would approve. Too abstract, even for gamers.

"A dedicated server sounds like a great idea to me. Anything you suggest. I really do appreciate your help on all that," Dave agreed.

"By the way." Carla leaned in toward the camera, her blouse gaping slightly in a way that reminded Dave to look *up*. "What the heck did you guys say to Sanders that made him go all Johnny Quest all of a sudden?"

Dave was confused. "I'm not sure what you mean—"

"Well, normally we don't see him much, he's kind of our boss's boss, and when we do see him he's all about 'profits are down,

122

we're spending too much, we need to learn to share toilet paper.' " Evan and Hank were nodding that they agreed. "Now, all of a sudden, it's like money is no object where you guys are concerned. Evan told you how he wasn't even allowed to take any time to clean up the code, and now Sanders has asked us to draw up job descriptions for extra headcount. Not that I'm complaining or anything, and not that we ever want the old guy back, but, seriously, what did you aliens do with *our* Sanders?"

Evan appeared to be desperately trying not to laugh, and Hank had already lost control. Dave spread his hands. "You got me. He did mention that this project had independent backing at DOD, so that must be it. Fresh money — he gets to expand his empire."

"But is it true he actually picked up your tab at the Hyatt?" she asked.

"Yeah, plus dinner and breakfast," Dave replied.

"Wow." Carla was absolutely stunned, like she was gazing at an actual alien. "Okay, new paradigm, I guess. Well, congratulations. Better ride that new pony while you still got it, guys."

"We will. Thanks. And thanks again for your help, guys," Dave answered. "Oops, and *gal*," he added, smiling.

"Ha! Nah, I'm still just one of the guys!" Carla shot back.

The conference call had come to an end, so they exchanged next steps and agreed to another call later in the week. Dave was pleased at how fast all of this was coming together, and the addition of Carla took a huge chunk of work off his plate. One that he was not going to miss, since he had little to no experience in the back end server environment. He made a note to mention the thing about Sanders and money to Marc. Probably nothing, but—

23

The week flew by quickly. Dave was engrossed in cleaning up the flight simulator source code, and by late Thursday he finally had it in good shape. He stripped out the demo code he had added earlier and sent a copy of the slimmed-down code out to Evan and Hank to use as the base for future development and maintenance of Prepar3D.

Meanwhile, Marc flew out to Seattle at the last minute to finish up the final vetting process for the developer application, which Sanders, true to his word, had gotten expedited. While he was out there, Marc had a chance to meet with the Xbox Ultimate launch team, who confirmed that their target launch window was now the first week in September. They also indicated that the full 120 fps 4k resolution spec was about 90 percent certain, but one of the team members confided to him privately that 90 percent was Microsoft code language for "almost 50 percent." Sanders had also arranged to bump Rocketship up to the top tier of candidates for an Ultimate beta console, due out in late spring.

After flying cross-country all Friday, and losing two time zones in the process, Marc got back to Austin late Friday afternoon. He was grinning ear-to-ear when he burst into the office and surprised Dave with a dozen DVDs full of documentation, sample code and support software for Xbox One development, plus five more DVDs for the Xbox Ultimate emulator and documentation.

Dave immediately scooped them up and started loading them on to the development computer.

With Dave giggling like a kid with a new toy, Marc decided to kick off for the rest of the day and head home to unpack. He buzzed Elle and suggested they grab dinner out, maybe at Mandola's Italian Market at The Triangle. The weather had turned warm, so sitting outside and people-watching over pasta seemed like a great idea.

Elle had spent the day working with her marketing team members on a presentation that was due in a few weeks, and she walked in the front door just as Marc was putting his suitcase away. They were now sharing a small house in a rapidly gentrifying neighborhood just north of Hancock and west of Burnet Road, and, after a quick smooch, they decided to take advantage of the good weather and bike to the restaurant.

Mandola's was crowded, as it always was on Friday nights, but Marc waited in line to place their orders while Elle trolled for a table outside. Marc ordered two glasses of wine, a Chianti for him and a chardonnay for Elle, and in twenty minutes they were both tucked into their food and halfway through their first drinks.

"So, we didn't get to talk much last night," Elle noted between bites. "How was your trip to Microsoft?"

"Actually, amazingly productive. That Sanders guy at Lockheed must have something on them, because the difference between CES and this week was night and day." Marc sat back, sipping on his Chianti. "We weren't getting any traction at all on our

126

developer application, and Dave was feeling pretty put out about it. But suddenly I walk in yesterday morning and it's like a conquering hero returning home. Unbelievable."

"So you got everything you needed?" she asked.

"That and a whole lot more. It was like they were willing to hand us the keys to the whole candy store. I even made the list for the first pre-production Xbox Ultimate consoles. I not only didn't see *that* coming, it wasn't even on our radar."

"How is Dave doing on the flight sim code?" Elle was ravenous and making short order of her plate of penne with vodka sauce.

"Actually, he's already a month ahead of the timelines we set over Christmas. He's got the code all cleaned up, and shipped a copy of the new, sleeker version out to the guys in Orlando. They were thrilled! It's something they'd been wanting to do for years, and Dave got it done in a week. Needless to say, they were pretty impressed."

"Sounds like you two had a good week," Elle mused.

"Really, a fantastic *two* weeks!" Marc replied. "I honestly felt Dave was close to packing it up after that trip to New York. You saw him, you know what he looked like. Then we make the trip to Florida and *bam!* We're flying at light speed all of a sudden."

"I'm really happy for you." Elle flashed him the little schoolgirl grin he loved so much. "Couldn't happen to a nicer couple of guys."

"Hey, nice guys finish last, doll," Marc grinned back. "With that in mind, what say we finish up here and head back to the house so I can show you my bad boy side?"

"I thought you'd never ask," she replied, polishing off the last bite of penne and reaching for her wine. "And don't forget to grab another bottle of wine for later."

"Consider it done," Marc responded, digging into his plate of veal marsala to catch up.

24

Dave begged Julia's forgiveness for working all weekend, but by the time Marc walked in on Monday morning, he already had most of the flight simulator code up and running on the Xbox.

"Hey, Marc, check this out." Dave moved the analog stick on the wireless controller and punched a button, and in seconds the Xbox display lit up with a man in blue jeans and white shirt walking across an airport tarmac toward a red-and-white Cessna 150 taildragger. Dave hit Pause and the action stopped.

"This is a canned scenario straight out of the Prepar3D database." Dave swung his seat around and tapped the keyboard on the development computer to wake it up. "Now let's play the very same scenario in the original PC-based software." He brought up the same scene on the computer and hit Play. "You see, exactly the same, except that the resolution on the Xbox is a lot lower, and the game box play is still kinda jumpy, 'cause I didn't have time yet to optimize the video calls and the avatar engine. Actually," Dave continued, popping up a YouTube video on the PC, "this is what the Prepar3D version looked like before I optimized the code—" He clicked a button on the YouTube screen, and the exact same scene began to play. As Marc watched, he noticed that the YouTube version was better than the Xbox version, but visibly less smooth than the version running on Dave's modified copy of Prepar3D.

"I got Evan on the line when he first walked into the office this morning in Orlando, and he was blown away at what a difference the new, streamlined code makes. I didn't tell him about the Xbox port, though. I thought I might give him a few more days, so he doesn't get his feelings hurt."

Marc agreed, pulling up another chair to get a better view of the action on the Xbox. "That's probably a good idea, but I think we *should* share this with Sanders. I have an update call scheduled with him this morning on Skype to brief him on the Seattle trip, and I'd really like to see the look on his face when I tell him what you've done in just one weekend."

"Okay, but let's not oversell it. That's the thing with programming. Sometimes everything just clicks, and other times you can get bogged down on the smallest things. I don't want to set any unrealistic expectations."

"Roger that," Marc agreed. "So, how much were you able to get working on Xbox?"

"Well, I had to back out some of the enhancements Lockheed made to Version 3 and Version 4, like the multiple monitor support and enhanced resolution, and of course their addition of a Windows 10 user interface had to be scrapped completely. The Xbox interface I'm using is actually very similar to the old Flight Simulator interface, except for the keyboard controls, where I'm going to have to work out some kind of simple mapping strategy—"

"I thought the Xbox could already use a keyboard and mouse. Wasn't that a feature Microsoft had to put in to let Xbox players compete with opponents going head-to-head against them on Windows 10?" Mark asked.

"Right, but we don't want to always assume the player has a keyboard attached, so we still need to map all of the most important functions to a standard Xbox controller or on-screen toggles," Dave explained.

"Okay, I get it. More of the old least common denominator tradeoffs. But go ahead, show me more." Marc was thrilled to see how much Dave had accomplished over the weekend, and he leaned in closer as Dave's avatar entered the plane, started it up and taxied down the runway. In moments the Cessna was airborne and climbing through the clouds.

"Ideally, you would want to use a joystick and flight pedals, or even a yoke and pedals, but that would add a lot of expense and complexity to the game, so we're stuck with relying on the standard controllers." Dave moved his thumb, and the aircraft banked to the left, still climbing. "If we were building a real port of Flight Simulator, our target market would be pilots, and they wouldn't hesitate to spend big bucks getting it to be as accurate as possible. In fact, there's a company that makes flight instrument add-ons for Flight Simulator, and you can easily blow a thousand or two building a customized cockpit. Down the road we might get into some of that, maybe for version two, but for version one we need to stick to the basics."

"Gotcha," Marc replied, dividing his attention between the action on the screen and Dave's fingers dancing on the controller. He made it all seem so easy, but Marc knew that much of it was due to the fact that Dave had been repeating the same motions and flying the same virtual plane for hours, making the code tighter and tighter to get it to this point. "So, Dave, before I talk to Sanders, what are the next steps on this? Would it be possible to do a demo for them sometime this week or next?"

Dave paused the action, turning away from the screen to face Marc. "Now that I've got it running, I need to loop back and turn on some of the functionality I stubbed out to get it working. Speeding up the video and the avatar generation will take maybe a day or two, and then I'll need to work up some kind of interface to replace what they stuck in for Windows 10. Actually, I'll need to scrunch up a whole new interface paradigm. This one is for a flight simulator, and where we really need to be heading is to figure out how the game is going to work."

"So, time frames? A week? Six weeks?"

"Give me the end of the week and I'll have the demo fully up and running on the Xbox at warp speed. I might even strap a few Hellfires onto this Cessna and take on an F-22." Dave grinned at the notion of that unlikely mismatch.

"I'll say two, just in case. Besides, after this weekend, you've got some making up to do with Jules—"

"I know. I promised her dinner at Uchi tonight."

"Uchi? Ouch! I love that place, but you can go broke trying to fill up on those tiny portions. Better grab a P.Terry on the way." P.Terry was a local Austin burger chain, similar in many ways to In-

N-Out Burger but with a certain Texas flair. Even coming from California, Marc had been a quick convert.

The Skype call with Sanders was still an hour off, so Marc left Dave to continue refining the Xbox simulation while he focused on finishing up his notes from the week before. By the time Sanders' face popped up on the screen of Marc's laptop, he'd changed his mind about sharing Dave's progress on the Xbox port. *Keep it in my back pocket for when I need it*, he thought. Instead he told Sanders about all the progress they had made at Microsoft, making sure to lavish ample praise on Sanders for all his help.

Marc did tell him about the code cleanup for Prepar3D, and how Dave had sent Evan and Hank a copy. He suggested walking Sanders through a demo of the new code versus the YouTube of the old code, but Sanders didn't sound at all interested.

"Yeah, I heard about all that from Nolan. Look, I need you boys to focus on the new software. Don't be wasting your time on that old Lockheed flight simulator stuff," he grumbled. "Stay on task."

"Well, Bob, Dave tells me he had to clean up the code first before he tacked all the new code onto it and moved it over to the Xbox. Sort of like you're better off cleaning the kitchen before starting to cook, or you'll reach for a pot and find it isn't there," Marc explained. Not the best analogy, but Sanders seemed to buy it.

"Okay, then, that's your call, but remember that I told our guys in Orlando that they need to jump through hoops for *you*, and not the other way around." Sanders glanced off-screen, like he was being interrupted by someone Marc couldn't see.

"Look, I gotta go. If you don't have anything else, let's make this a regular for Monday mornings. Nine all right for you?"

Nine was a little early for Marc, as he usually liked to get up after sunrise and have breakfast with Elle, but he wasn't going to argue about it. Not with the guy who had just ordered his own people to jump through hoops for the project. "Nine is great. So unless something big comes up before then, we'll talk in a week."

Sanders reached over and closed the call. Marc was left staring at the screen and wondering what the guy from Lockheed was really thinking. Sanders was so hard to read. *A riddle*, he muttered to himself, *wrapped in a mystery, inside an enigma.*

25

The reports from CIA's North Korea desk were startling. Everything seemed to be unraveling so fast that even the intelligence agencies couldn't keep pace with developments. The President stood up impatiently and turned to stare out the window at the White House front lawn. "Jim, we're running out of time."

White House Chief of Staff Jim Staunton walked over to stand beside his boss. He hadn't read the reports, but he knew what was in them. The Korean peninsula was in the throes of a multi-year drought. For South Korea, that meant a marked increase in food imports, which translated into a windfall for American farmers. But for the Democratic People's Republic of Korea, locked behind its own self-imposed version of the Iron Curtain, imports weren't an option.

And North Korea was already in the middle of the barley hump, the lean season before the summer harvest of rice and corn arrived. Even in the best of times the population would be starving. World Food Program estimates showed that the North Korean diet provided 25% less protein and 30% less fat than what was required to sustain a healthy life. And now they were facing a repeat of the so-called arduous march of the 1990's, when millions of North Koreans died from malnutrition. This time, unless some miracle occurred, the entire country of North Korea would be looking like a Nazi concentration camp by the time the summer crops were harvested. And unless the drought ended soon, even those crops would probably fail.

"What do you think is going to happen to them?" Staunton asked, noting the deep grimace on the President's face.

"Well, Jim, for once all the intelligence agencies are in agreement. They have no idea. The DPRK's Supreme Leader is afraid of an uprising, so he's clamping down pretty hard on his people, hard even for him. But there's only so much pressure you can apply before the country pops wide open. If that starts to happen, there are two likely possibilities, neither of them good." The President turned to face the Chief of Staff, his right hand resting heavily on the chair beside him. "One, everything collapses, and the warlords take over. One or more of them takes possession of the country's nukes. Then we have to worry about dealing with them, or maybe some other power that rises up to buy the nukes off of them. Like ISIS." He paused for a moment, turning again to stare out the window at the crowds of tourists gathered on the other side of the White House gates. "Two, the Supreme Leader panics as his world starts spinning apart, and decides to lob one of his nukes over the DMZ and into South Korea. Or, for that matter, at us. Either way, this is the most dangerous scenario for a possible nuclear disaster since the Cuban Missile Crisis. And unlike Kennedy, I don't have anyone rational to talk to on the other side."

"How much time do we have?" Staunton asked softly, the frightening implications of the President's predictions beginning to sink in.

"Hard to say, Jim. Weeks. Months, maybe. But not long. Not long at all."

"So what can we do?"

"We can pray, Jim. Pray for rain for the Korean peninsula. And pray that Sanders can deliver Beekeeper in time."

26

Dave had promised to have the demo fully ported to the Xbox by the end of the week. In fact, he got it done by the end of Tuesday, and then moved on to fleshing out the other elements of the game.

A large part of his success was due to the fact that the preferred development environment for programming Xboxes was Visual Studio, the same tool Dave was using for the Prepar3D code. Microsoft Visual Studio was an integrated development environment used to develop computer programs for Microsoft Windows, in addition to web sites, web applications, web services, and, of course, Xbox. Programmers could edit the code in Visual Studio, and then, with a single click, compile and debug the code. As a result, Dave was able to cut and paste code from Prepar3D directly into the Xbox *Dronewars* code, make quick modifications, and then compile and test the changes.

By the time the weekend rolled around, almost all of the major features of the game had been roughed out. At least well enough that Dave could start tinkering with the look and feel of the game, how the game would actually be played. And that was why he was facing his first big hurdle.

"I've worked out most of the first person controls, how to fly a drone or a jet toward a target and blow things up. I've even got that working reliably in full 1080p resolution," he explained to Marc, walking him through various aspects of the game. "And as you can see, I've roughed out the third person screens, where you can view all of the threats around you and all of the target opportunities—" Dave pushed a button and the view flipped to a radar-type screen covered with variously colored shapes, with the outline of an airplane at the very center of the screen.

"That is absolutely amazing, Dave. And the realism is way off the charts, especially this early on. So, where's the problem?" Marc asked.

"Well, the problem is, at this point all I have is static targets. I can move them around somewhat using a randomizer, and I can even put elements like anti-aircraft fire in place, also driven by a randomizer, but to get to the next level I need an intelligence on the other side driving my opponent's actions. I can fake it by using a robotic opponent, but that really isn't what this game is all about." Dave sat back with a noticeable sigh.

"Okay," Marc offered, "so what do we need to do to solve it?"

"Well, the thing is, I need at least a half-time person to play the commies, so I can test out the changes I'm making in game play, plus we're going to need to move ahead on the back end server. We've gotten to the point where the Prepar3D back end is barely being used by the game. We need a whole new set of code on the server side to coordinate the online interaction between the players. And, where the Prepar3D server had fairly limited numbers of objects it needed to juggle at one time, maybe two to five aircraft running the same formation simulation, now we're talking about tracking hundreds, maybe thousands of sprites at the same time, and handling split-second collision detection on all of them."

Marc was stroking his chin absentmindedly. "You lost me there, buddy. Why so many?"

"Because you not only have to track all of the drones and planes in the air, and other targets and shooters on the ground, but also all of the munitions that are being tossed back and forth by each and every one of them. The Predators, as you know, are generally armed with two Hellfire missiles. But when you look at the A-10 Warthog, it carries a 30mm, seven-barrel GAU-8/A Avenger cannon in its nose that can hold as many as 1,200 rounds, and fires at a rate of almost four thousand rounds per minute. In other words, hold down the fire button on the A-10 for just ten seconds and you've got over six hundred bullets to track. From just one aircraft."

"Right, now I see the problem. Then scale that times the number of active aircraft per player, then the number of players online at the same time, and that's one heck of a lot of objects flying around at one time." Marc was trying to work through the math to get a sense of just how much horsepower they would need on the back end, but gave up. He just knew it was a really big number. "So, again, what do we need to do to solve it?"

"This is way above my pay grade," Dave admitted. "At this point, we're going to need to put the back end on the front burner. And while I might be able to mush my way through all of that, I have almost zero experience in that field, and absolutely zero experience on the hardware side, on the high-end server arrays we're gonna need to run this."

"I guess that's where Carla comes in," Marc suggested. "Well, you've got a week out there in Orlando with nothing better to do, so maybe she'll have some ideas on how to move forward. In the meantime, I'll see what I can do to recruit one of Elle's colleagues from the business school to be your doppelgänger." Marc had a funny thought. "The last time I was over at the McCombs School, Elle took me up to the graduate lounge, and they have this giant sculpture of a hammer sitting there, I suppose symbolizing capitalism in some abstract way. Maybe we can steal it, bring it over here and super glue a sickle to it. That could be your opponent's symbol, a commie hammer and sickle!"

"Just my luck," muttered Dave. "My partner is a felon with a fifth-grade sense of humor—"

27

As they had planned just two weeks earlier, Dave headed out to Orlando on Sunday afternoon, arriving just before sunset. He grabbed a room at the Residence Inn, using some of the Marriott points he had saved up while working at Google.

When he showed up at Lockheed on Monday morning, he was pleasantly surprised to find that they had issued him a contractor's badge. And he even had a small office, just down the hall from Evan, Hank and Carla, who he finally got to meet in person. After letting him settle in for a bit, Evan and Hank drug him off to the same conference room they had used weeks before. A box of donuts and a pot of coffee were already waiting, and Dave dug into a chocolate glazed donut with abandon. *Julia would never let me bring that kind of sugar-laced poison into our house,* he thought. *Ah, the benefits of being on the road.*

Evan had set up an Xbox, plugged into the big screen monitor, and was quickly booting it up.

"So, what's the story with Sanders?" Dave asked, smears of chocolate already caking his lips. "I mean, not to look a gift horse in the mouth, but he doesn't really seem like the type to be running a software company. At least not something that's as consumer oriented as Prepar3D."

Evan and Hank exchanged a quick look. "We-e-ell, he's kind of new around here," Evan began.

"What do you mean?" Dave asked.

Hank eyed Dave warily. He had been through an awful lot of office politics at Microsoft, and the back stabbing at Lockheed made the Microsoft boys seem like amateurs. Still, he trusted Dave. And it felt good to have another person around to trust. "He got here, what, maybe seven, eight months ago?" Evan indicated that seemed about right. "Replaced a fellow who had been here from the very start of the program, Nick Teller. We were in the middle of the Version 4 launch at the time, and Nick stayed on to see it through, but then, *poof*, he was gone and Sanders was in. And we were never told what happened to Nick, or why. He was just gone, like overnight."

Evan piped in. "As for Sanders, he is even more of a mystery. Nobody's ever heard of him. We checked the Lockheed personnel listings. Nothing. We Googled him. Again nothing. He's like a ghost, just magically appearing out of the mist."

Interesting, Dave thought. "What does he do around here? Is he a coder? Does he come from a simulation background?"

Again the quick, wary glance. "Actually, other than being a bastard about budgets, he's been pretty hands off, so we really don't know anything about him, other than the fact that he's the boss," Evan explained. "After the V4 launch, and until you guys showed up, we've mainly been focused on bug fixes, and occasionally getting a new corporate customer up to speed, but Sanders never got involved. He has an office here, but we very seldom ever saw him. Whatever he was working on, whatever he was actually doing around here, he kept all of that close to the vest."

"And then you guys showed up for that meeting, and things changed," Hank continued. "I think I've seen more of him in the last few weeks than in all the time we've been working for him. And where we used to get hassled for nickels and dimes, now he's tossing around twenties and hundreds. It's like all of a sudden we woke up, and we're working for a new company."

"Well, I guess I should say you're welcome, guys," Dave grinned, breaking the mood. Just at that moment, Carla walked into the conference room, a 17-inch laptop in tow.

"Morning, boys," she purred, emphasizing the word "boys." Dave liked the way she filled out her tight skirt, something that hadn't been evident in the Skype calls. But even as he was subtly ogling her body, Dave noticed an equally subtle shift in the air. Evan and Hank had gone very quiet. Not just that they weren't saying anything. Just *quiet*. Something about Carla. Dave made a mental note to keep track of her. Google had its share of backstabbing professionals, too.

28

But Carla turned out to be very easy to work with, and she had a good grasp of the server issues, particularly on the hardware side. *Dronewars* would need a solidly robust server array, with plenty of redundancy. It wouldn't do to have a few thousand players kicked out of the game all of a sudden because of a server blip. Carla assured Dave that she could have a server room fully implemented and tested well before launch, assuming the resources were there.

"How much is that going to cost?" Dave asked.

"That's kind of a function of how many users you see coming online at the same time. And we'll want to budget in some level of extra capacity so we can scale up into a bigger traffic load without having to bring the game down to swap out new equipment. I'd say, since this is mostly an in-memory application with limited disk traffic, we can go with a blade server approach, loaded up with extra RAM, and a RAID 5 solid state disk array to save state information. How many players do you think you'll have at launch?"

Dave thought about that. "At the very start, if we had twenty thousand I'd be happy. Cap it at fifty thousand, and I think we'd have our bases covered."

"Okay." Carla did some quick calculations in her head. "From my experience, with the new blades on the market, we should be able to handle five thousand users per blade. That's ten blades for the upside, plus another ten blades to mirror the first ten. That way,

145

we'd have a hot swap capability. If a server went down, the game would continue on its mirrored server with almost no noticeable delay. And, of course, we'd need a few spares of everything to swap back in for anything that failed and got pulled out."

Dave thought that sounded about right, but he had very little experience in the area, so he had to go with Carla's judgment.

"Add in a rack to hold everything, which dollar-wise is nothing, and a KVM switch so we only need one monitor and keyboard to cover all the servers, then add in the fattest router you can afford, and we're looking at an equipment cost between a hundred and a hundred fifty. Thousand."

Ouch, Dave thought. Every time they turned around, it was another big bill to pay. As Everett Dirksen once famously said about the federal budget, a billion here and a billion there, and pretty soon you're talking real money. Dave wondered when all of this hemorrhaging was going to end.

Carla wasn't finished. "You're also going to need a dedicated server room, with a solid uninterruptible power supply, good A/C, and a fire suppression system. And some way to lay a fat pipe to a trunk line for the Internet. There are a lot of collocation facilities spread around that can handle that for you for a fee, but the downside is they are usually located somewhere pretty inconvenient, so monitoring and managing is a huge hassle. If you can pull it off, I would suggest having your own server room, ideally somewhere near a major hospital."

"Why is that important?" Dave wondered.

"It's all about the power grid, Dave. Think about all the times the power has gone out on you, and you're stuck at home with no lights, everything slowly melting in the fridge. Even the best battery-based uninterruptible power supply will only cover you for an hour or so, but you can't afford to let a lightning strike in Austin, Texas, shut down your game in Omaha, Nebraska. And if you have a situation like they had in California in the late '90s, where Pacific Gas and Electric implemented rolling blackouts across major cities like Los Angeles and San Diego, you're screwed."

Carla continued. "But hospitals, especially Level 1 trauma centers, the power companies can't let them go dark. That section of the grid always gets priority. It doesn't get blacked out, and if there is a power failure, that's the first part of the grid to get fixed. Does Austin have a medical center cluster, an area where all the major hospitals are located?"

"Yeah," Dave responded, drawing a mental map of the east campus area. "Just north of downtown along the west side of the interstate. The new medical school, with a hospital and tons of medical offices, and St. Davids. And the Dell Children's Hospital is not far away."

"There you go. And what about Internet access? Is there a major trunk line close by?"

Dave thought about it. "As I understand it, one of the core Internet backbones runs right through the UT campus, to a facility they have hidden away in an old building on the east side of campus I don't know how we could get access to that, though."

147

"Have Marc bring it up with Sanders," Carla suggested. "Those trunk lines all started as DARPA facilities. He might have a DOD connection that could help you out." The Defense Advanced Research Projects Agency was the part of the Department of Defense responsible for development of emerging technologies for use by the military. The modern commercial Internet actually started as a DARPA project intended to improve the ability of scientists and engineers involved in military research to communicate and share files. Most of the original ARPANET installations were located on university campuses, where the scientists had also served as professors.

"Not a bad idea," Dave agreed. "On a related note, I know you can help us get the server array going, but what about the software? You already have a lot on your hands just keeping Prepar3D up and running. I can't see you having the time to modify your back end server code to meet our needs. And I don't have the knowledge to make that happen, at least not in the time frame we need this to happen."

"Well, I'll talk to Nolan about it, and that might be something else for Marc to bring up with Sanders." Carla was knitting her brow, pensive. "I *do* know some guys out there we might be able to steal if we had the money, but for a high-risk operation like yours, it would either have to be *big* money, or some chunk of the action. No one is going to walk away from a solid, good paying job unless there is some serious upside to it."

"Okay," Dave agreed. "You handle Nolan, I'll take it up with Marc, and we'll see what we can do. At the end of the day, we don't have a lot of choice. Without the server, *Dronewars* is just another me-too first person shooter, even with the extra realism I was able to squeeze in. So whatever it takes, we'll have to bite the bullet and do it. Whatever it costs."

29

With limited resources to make much immediate progress on the server problem, Dave decided to move up his plane ticket and return to Austin on Thursday afternoon. He would have left even earlier, but Evan and Hank convinced him to let them buy lunch as a partial thank you for cleaning up the source code. They also invited Carla, but she had a conflict and begged off.

Lunch was a tropically-themed hamburger restaurant located not far from Lockheed. The restaurant offered a variety of hamburger combinations, like a burger with ham and pineapple, but the main draw seemed to be a pile of french fries with chili and grated cheese. Evan ordered a large portion of the fries to share, but Dave thought they looked like a heart attack just waiting to happen and tried only a couple just to be polite.

While they were waiting for their burgers to arrive, Dave once again brought up the topic of the various players in the Lockheed organization. He had been a bit surprised to see that Peter Nolan — Evan, Hank and Carla's boss — was so clearly hands off in regards to the new project. And Nolan didn't seem to object to the fact that Dave was eating up so much of their time. In fact, Dave got the sense that Nolan was actually going out of his way to avoid him.

"So what is it with your boss Nolan?" Dave asked, grabbing another chili-coated fry and popping it into his mouth.

"What do you mean?" Hank asked. "Has he been a problem?"

"No," Dave replied. "Quite the opposite. He's nice enough when I talk to him, and he's been great as far as getting me all set up out here. But it seems strange that he is so disengaged in what we're doing. Like there's some kind of wall separating him from the new project. And Sanders even made a point, really, of making sure everyone knew Marc was working directly with him, and I was working with you guys. Cutting Nolan out of the picture almost entirely."

"Well, hmmm." Evan thought about it a second. "We don't really have any visibility to that. I know Nolan was very pleased with the code cleanup you did, particularly when he saw what it did to smooth out the simulation. Thanks again for that, by the way." Dave waved it off as nothing. "You know, ever since Nick left — or got canned, or whatever happened — and Sanders came in, Nolan and Sawyer have been pretty much running the show around here. Both of them have been around forever, and other than the new version releases, there hasn't been a lot of drama around here. It's just the same old thing, day in and day out."

Evan glanced over at Hank. "But, again, you guys show up, and now all that's changed. It's like Nolan and Sawyer are afraid of something, afraid to interfere. Even this week, when we're supposed to be working on fixing a bug that's popping up with the new nVidia graphics card but instead we're off doing stuff with you, it's all no worries, mate. Not normal." Hank indicated that he agreed.

151

"How about Carla?" Dave asked, noting the same dangerous look flash between Evan and Hank that he had seen earlier in the week.

Hank hesitated. "Carla is something of an unknown. She came in shortly after Sanders. No interview that we were aware of, which is strange, because normally we would have had to buy off on any new team member."

"And she's nice enough," Evan added. "And extremely capable, almost overqualified for the kind of work she's doing. But after all these months, while on the surface she's very friendly, at the same time certain things just don't seem to add up. It's like she's hiding something."

"We're all hiding something," Dave suggested.

"Yeah," Hank kicked in, "but it's more than that. Maybe part of it is that she seems to have some kind of... *familiarity* with Sanders. Nothing obvious, it's just you get the sense that they know each other from somewhere else. Like Sanders will say something, and Evan and I have no idea what he's talking about, but she does. She *gets* it."

"Maybe it's just that Hank and I are pretty thick," Evan suggested dismissively. "Maybe we've just been together so long it's like inbreeding. We've gone socially stupid."

Or maybe not. Dave decided once again that he needed to keep an eye on Carla, just in case.

30

Storms had popped up across the southern United States, delaying flights by several hours. Dave's flight didn't land at Austin Bergstrom until almost midnight, so he went straight home, giving Julia a quick peck on the cheek before sliding between the covers.

The next morning, he and Marc agreed to meet for breakfast at The Omelettry on Airport Boulevard. Dave ordered the Popeye omelet with gingerbread pancakes. Marc just had a stack of buttermilk banana pancakes with coffee. Over breakfast, Dave walked Marc through everything that had happened in Orlando, including the concerns about server costs and additional headcount, but left off bringing up his reservations regarding Carla and the overall atmosphere at Lockheed. He needed more information on that subject before getting Marc all worried about it.

Marc suggested that Dave put together a brief memo, just a page or so, and he would shoot it over to Sanders in advance of their regular Monday morning call. "We're not going to let money be the hang-up, Dave, especially after everything you've done so far to move this project forward. If we need some more people, we'll get them, even if I have to pay for it myself."

"No," Dave quickly responded. "We're partners, so if we need to spend the money, we'll do it together. I just wanted you to know what we're facing. I'm really excited about where this is headed, and I'm on board as far as reaching into my pocket to help pay for more help. But you're the guy doing the numbers and the business plan, so I need to let you know about any of these roadblocks as soon as I come across them."

Marc smiled and chomped on a heaping forkful of his pancakes, the syrup dripping down across his plate en route to his mouth. "Well, remember that Lockheed is in this, too, and the server issue affects them as much as it does us. So I'll hit up Sanders on Monday and see if he can't spring for some extra discretionary cash. Meanwhile, get back with Carla about those names she has. I'd like to move on this as fast as possible, because we can't afford for you to be sitting idle waiting for the server piece to get up and running."

"Thanks, Marc. By the way, any luck with those B-school guys you thought might want to moonlight as my opposing players?"

"Elle hit them up with it on Tuesday, after class. They were all busy getting ready for team presentations in marketing, so she didn't get a firm answer yet. But it appears they were pretty eager to help out."

"Super. Even without the extra headcount I think I can have a rudimentary server capability up in a week or so. It would be great to have at least one person available by then." Dave dug back in to his omelet, pushing a bite of spinach and egg around the plate to drag up some more hollandaise sauce. It was great working with someone like Marc who could just get things done for a change.

31

Marc started to raise the issue of the server costs on his Monday morning call, but Sanders stopped him with a raised hand. "I got the memo on Friday, and had a chance to talk it over with Nolan. It's pretty clear from what Elliott has already done that's he's no slacker. If this is what he thinks he needs to get the job done, then let's do it. Just shoot me the numbers, and as long as they don't break the bank, I'll give you a go-ahead by the end of the week. But remember that all I'm committing to is salaries through launch, then it's on you. And any bonus promises or stock options you have to throw in to get whoever you need, those are on you, too."

"Thanks, Bob. That's a load off my chest. I'll get those numbers out to you as soon as we hang up."

"Fine. And let me be frank with you. Part of this is that I'm coming under a lot of heat to expedite this project."

Mark nodded warily. "And by expedite you mean—"

"Look, son, I take it you watch the news. Or whatever you guys do on the Internet to stay up with what's happening in the world?" Sanders' eyes narrowed.

"Of course. I read the tablet version of the *Austin American-Statesman* every morning before work."

"Good, then you know this planet is going into the shitter in a hurry." Sanders tapped his index finger on the desk in front of him for emphasis. "Damn thing's falling apart all around us. The Ukraine

155

is on the verge of collapse. Russia's running what they claim are 'exercises' all along their southern border with Europe, and making territorial moves on the thawing Arctic Ocean. The Chinese have doubled the size of their navy and are steaming up and down the South China Sea and off the coast of Japan and South Korea. We still have those damned Arabs to worry about in Syria and Iraq. And everyone's calling on the President to do something about it."

"Yes, sir, I'm aware of all that," Marc responded. "But what does any of that have to do with us?"

"Well, the Pentagon has been asked in no uncertain terms to fix this. Which means they've asked me in even tougher language to fix the part I'm responsible for. And now I'm *telling* you we need to move up our timetables for the war games software—" Sanders fixed Marc with a glare that left no doubt how that sentence ended. *And no questions asked!*

Marc's head was spinning. This had come completely out of left field. "What kind of target date are we talking?"

32

H e said *what*?" Dave was apoplectic when he heard the news, and Marc really couldn't blame him..

"Hey, Dave, he agreed to give us all the resources we need to get it done, including setting us up in a real office so we have room for everybody." Marc was desperately trying to smooth things out, but Dave appeared completely distraught. And for good reason.

"July *first?*" Dave stalked furiously around the office, shaking his head and slamming his fist on the top of a desk in anger. "July *first?* What the *hell!*"

"Calm down, Dave."

"I'm not calming down. I *knew* something like this would happen. We let 'em stick their nose in the tent an inch, and suddenly they've taken over!" Dave picked up a C++ manual and chucked it across the room, narrowly missing the new 32-inch monitor for the Xbox.

"They're not taking over, Dave. Look, calm down and let's talk about this."

"What's to talk about? One moment this is *our* company, *our* project, and now they're bossing us around like they're goddamned programming mafia! Like they know what it takes to code this goddamned game! It's been one month, *one month*, and now Sanders is *our* boss! Evan, Hank, Carla, and now *us!*"

"That's not what this is about, Dave, and you know it." Marc was exasperated. "Look, we went to them and asked for help, not the other way around. A month ago and this company was on the ropes, we were pretty much out of options. And they've given us those options, Dave! Now we have the people and the money to really make this work."

"But July *first?*"

"It's just two months sooner than we thought, Dave. And, truthfully, if the guys from Microsoft were planning to launch Xbox Ultimate in mid-summer, you would be the first person pushing to be ready for that launch. Plus, Sanders has promised us a lot more in exchange for moving up our launch date. A *lot* more."

"Like what?" Dave was still madder than hell, but at least he was listening.

"Well, first of all, he really wanted us to be ready with *Warg* July first, and push off *Dronewars* until later. I finally convinced him that, from a programming perspective, *Dronewars* had to come first. *Warg* is built on *Dronewars*, not vice versa." Marc managed to pull off that story with a straight face. No small feat, even for him.

"Not exactly true, but go on," Dave said.

"Second, I told him there was no way we could make that date happen with the resources we have in place today, even with the extra programmers for the back end server. And he could go straight to hell if he thought you and I were going to dip further into our Google savings to save *his* ass."

Dave had to laugh at that. He could just see Sanders' face when Marc dropped *that* line on him.

"So we compromised. It's not ideal, but it's a compromise. And it gets us — gets *you* — a whole lot more resources to help you pull this off."

"Again, what kind of resources?" Dave was starting to come around.

"To begin with, pretty much as many people as we need. As *you* need." Marc held up his hand. "And I know, before you start lecturing me on the mythical man month, I know we can't just throw bodies at this thing to get it done. But I also know that our schedule has just shifted from a little over seven months to a little over five months, so you can't tell me more manpower can't make a difference."

The fire was slowly going out of Dave's eyes. He could do the math, too, and maybe this wasn't as bad as he had first thought. Maybe he *might* have overreacted a bit. "I'm also going to need a lot of help in converting their CAD files of vehicles and weapons systems into our file structure."

"Yeah, I told him that. *And* I told him we needed a hell of a lot more space for all those new faces, plus a state-of-the-art server room." Marc chuckled. "I figured, while I had him on the ropes, now was the time to go for the gold."

"And he was okay with that?"

"Well, I won't say there wasn't a bit of frank discussion going back and forth." Mark paused. "Okay, *heated* discussion." He

159

laughed a bit, slapping Dave playfully on the shoulder. "But he doesn't have much choice, does he? A few minutes ago you said Sanders was taking over. The problem for him is, he's not really in the driver's seat for this. We are, because there is absolutely no way this is going to happen anywhere close to his deadlines unless we make it happen."

Dave clearly hadn't been thinking about their relationship with Lockheed in that way, but the new revelation that he and Marc held the upper hand, and not the other way around, brought a slow smile to his face. "Marc, I have to apologize for blowing up at you. I acted like a child, like I didn't trust you, but you've had my back the whole way. I'm sorry, man. You're a true friend."

Marc shook it off. "Nah, I totally understand. I was there in that very same place when Sanders broke the news to me. And by the way, we have each *other's* back. You and me, buddy. We're going to shock the world together!"

33

Mahmoud Abdulaziz pulled slowly into the parking garage off Kettner Boulevard. He was driving a tan Mitsubishi Outlander, rented from a company in Windsor, Canada, and driven across the border by a female convert to the cause from western Oregon. Once the SUV was safely across the border, with its precious cargo still tucked discretely into false panels in the sides of the car, Abdulaziz rendezvoused with the woman and continued the trip south to San Diego alone.

Retrieving a parking ticket from the machine at the entrance, he continued up the ramp to the top floor of the parking structure. He parked as far south as he could, close to the steady stream of airplanes taking off from Runway 9, then popped open the rear hatch and stepped out of the car.

Normally, all aviation traffic at San Diego International Airport landed from the east, on Runway 27. It was actually the same physical runway as Runway 9 — the different runway designations simply indicated the compass direction of the landing aircraft. Runway 27 pointed to the west, at a compass heading of 270 degrees, while Runway 9 pointed due east at a heading of 90 degrees. The preference for Runway 27 was based upon several factors, including noise restrictions, terrain, and, most importantly, the fact that prevailing winds generally came off the ocean from the west.

Today, however, all that had changed. An unseasonable Santa Anna wind was blowing in from the deserts to the east of the city, forcing the airport to switch to east-bound departures. *Allah is merciful*, he thought, eyeing the congested area just east of the airport. Sweeping his eyes carefully over the area to make sure he wasn't being observed, he opened the latches on the large case in the rear of the Outlander and quickly began to assemble the parts inside. That took only a few minutes. He carefully pushed everything back inside the car and out of view, covering his cargo with a large blanket, and then stepped back to consider his targets.

The parking garage was located almost exactly two blocks from the end of Runway 9. The noise from the departing planes was deafening as they roared overhead, seemingly just a fingertip's distance away. Abdulaziz watched as one by one they pulled onto the far end of the runway, throttled up and hurtled toward him, pulling up at the last possible moment to clear the fence at the very end. After departing the airport, they turned slightly to the left or right, depending upon their eventual destination. Abdulaziz waited patiently. *I want a big one,* he thought. *A 747 at least.*

Less than ten minutes later his patience was rewarded. An American Airlines 747 pulled onto the runway, ultimately bound for Hawaii by way of Phoenix Sky Harbor. Checking once more for prying eyes, he raised the hatch of his SUV and pulled out the weapon.

The FIM-92A Stinger was a shoulder-mounted infrared homing surface-to-air missile. The missile had originally been given

162

to a Syrian rebel group by the United States Army, then quickly made its way into the hands of the Islamic State. It was approximately five feet long and three inches in diameter. The missile by itself weighed 22 pounds — 34 pounds including its launcher. When fired, a small ejection motor shot the missile out of the mouth of the launcher before firing its two-stage solid-fuel rocket, which then accelerated it to a speed of Mach 2.54, almost three thousand feet per second. At maximum speed, the rocket would cover a mile in less than two seconds. Mounted on the nose of the rocket was a 3 kg penetrating hit-to-kill warhead. After firing, the missile is designed to lock on to the heat signature of a target aircraft's engines. The FIM-92A was an older version of the weapon, and could be fooled by normal anti-missile countermeasures, such as flairs. Unfortunately for AA Flight 568, even if the aircraft had been equipped with anti-missile defenses, the short distances involved today would have given the pilot no time to use them.

He inserted a battery coolant unit into the launcher's hand guard, blasting a stream of argon gas into the system and firing off a chemical energy charge that powered up the missile and its infrared targeting device. The American Airlines 747 was racing down the runway in front of him, its nose just starting to rotate up. He fought the urge to fire at this point. *Not yet. All the more glory if I wait.* The aircraft's wheels eased off the pavement and began to rotate into the wheel wells in the nose and wings of the plane. He aimed the launcher with his right eye, his left eye squeezed tightly shut. In seconds, the plane roared overhead. *Almost there.* The plane was past him, already starting its bank toward the right. Abdulaziz took a deep breath, letting it out with a soft prayer. *Bismillah Arrahman Arraheem. In the name of Allah, the most gracious, the most merciful.* His finger softly and gently squeezed the trigger.

34

Alfalfa Heavy 568, cleared for departure Runway Oh-Niner." The pilot could hear faint laughter from the tower controllers in the background.

"Alpha Alpha 568, departing Runway Oh-Niner," the pilot answered back with just a hint of annoyance. By tradition, air traffic control assigned call signs for all the major airlines using the military alphabet translation of the first letters of the airline's name, then tacking on the official flight number. For United Airlines, for example, the call signs started with Uniform Alpha, for UA. For American Airlines, or AA, the controllers invariably contracted the Alpha Alpha to Alfalfa, a practice American Airlines pilots greatly disliked. But the more the pilots pushed back, the more widespread the practice became, and it was now a fully institutionalized joke within the aviation community.

The 747 pulled onto the runway, lining up with the center stripe. Running a quick final sweep of the instruments, the pilot pushed the throttle quadrant forward and the plane responded, sluggishly at first but then rapidly gaining speed. At rotation speed he pulled the yoke back and the nose lifted. A few seconds later the back tires eased off the runway as well, and the plane was airborne. The 747 easily cleared the crash fence at the end of the runway, then roared over the parking garage just beyond, the landing gear indicator showing that the wheels were almost fully retracted. The pilot reached over to toggle the radio to Departure Control, and initiated a gentle bank to the right. With his visibility limited to the front of the aircraft, he never saw the missile as it was launched from behind him at point-blank range.

Normally, the Stinger missile would have targeted the aircraft's primary heat source, its engines. By a fluke, however, the impact occurred on the left horizontal stabilizer, the fins sticking out on either side of the tail. The warhead stuck a glancing blow and detonated almost on top of the stabilizer, just to the left of the tail. As a result, much of the energy from the blast missed the aircraft, saving the tail section from instantaneous disintegration. Almost immediately, though, the right wing of the plane drooped and its nose dipped sharply as the air pressure normally pushing down on the left stabilizer dropped off significantly. There was just very little horizontal stabilizer left for the air to push down on.

The pilot heard the sharp report of the explosion, and suddenly the plane started to corkscrew to the right, its nose plummeting alarmingly. Working together, the pilot and copilot fought to bring the plane level, pulling back on their respective yokes with all their strength to raise the nose, while turning the yokes sharply to the left to correct the right bank. For a moment, their efforts seemed to be working. The pilot thumbed his microphone. "Mayday! Mayday!" he shouted out to SoCal Departure Control. But that was all of the message he got out. The left stabilizer, already heavily damaged, couldn't handle the additional strain being placed on it by the pilots' emergency maneuvers. In seconds it sheared completely off the aircraft, tumbling to the ground just a few hundred feet below, narrowly missing a small car. Once again, the plane banked sharply to the right and dropped its nose, the bank developing quickly into a full corkscrew as the aircraft fell from the sky. The airplane barely cleared the Horton Plaza shopping center, but then crashed squarely into the northern face of the Marriott Marquis San Diego Marina resort on West Harbor Drive, still full of fuel and with more than 500 souls on board.

all systems go for launch

35

Just locating all of the bodies from the crash and resulting explosion took several weeks, with all of the world in mourning for the 1,173 victims who were finally identified and laid to rest. In a repeat of the events of 9/11, FAA and Homeland Security ordered a shutdown of the entire United States civil aviation system.

But this time the country rebounded more quickly. FAA and Homeland realized that little could be done to prevent similar attacks in the future, other than moving all of the country's 5,145 public airports to remote locations that could be more tightly monitored and protected. The President delivered a stirring but tremulous speech from the site of the disaster, a speech heard around the world. "The sad truth is, terrorists are like cockroaches. No matter how many you kill, it always seems there are even more waiting, hiding in the dark crevasses to crawl out and attack when any opportunity arises. But we cannot give up, we cannot let them win. We must be ever vigilant, always ready to crush them out of existence beneath our boots. Every chance we get. And that means we must redouble our efforts, as a nation, yea as a world, to eradicate radical Islam wherever it exists, and eradicate our enemies who breed those cockroaches and release them into our midst. This country will not — *can* not — forget what happened in San Diego. We must use this moment as a clarion call for freeing our world from this awful menace. I pledge to you this night that henceforth the United States will dedicate all of its energy, all of its might, to light up those dark crevasses and bring our enemies to justice. We cannot relax one moment until each and every one of us are once again safe from this evil. Until once again this planet is at peace."

Back at Rocketship headquarters, the next month went by quickly, albeit in a much more somber state of mind. Marc located some office space in a converted two-story house just east of Interstate 35, near all the hip new restaurants on Manor Road. They decided to use the downstairs rooms for business and marketing, turning the original kitchen into a break room. A large windowless upstairs room was dedicated to the new back end servers and other electronic support equipment, while the rest of the upstairs became shared space for Dave and the new development staff.

Carla was a big help in locating and hiring that staff, and, when it became obvious that she couldn't manage the accelerated implementation of the back end servers from out in Orlando, Sanders agreed to have her transfer to Austin for the duration. She still had general responsibilities for managing the back end of Prepar3D, but that work had wound down following the successful launch of Version 4, so she felt comfortable handling it all from Austin with an occasional trip back to Florida.

By early March the program was really starting to take shape. With help from Lockheed and DOD, Dave made great strides in converting the CAD files for the various weapons, aircraft, ships and land vehicles for NATO forces, although he was still struggling with the less detailed models for opposition forces. Dave also developed a

172

rudimentary back end server to test the game, but when Carla and the new programmers took a look they decided to scrap Dave's code and start all over again from scratch.

Dave's back end code *was* useful, though, for helping Marc walk through some early focus group tests, put together using mostly University of Texas students, with a great deal of help from Elle. It was during one such focus group, held on a Thursday night just a week before the trip to Dallas, that they uncovered the first big stumbling block in their game design. The session ran late into the night, and Marc needed some time the next morning to organize his thoughts and formalize his notes, so he called Dave and they agreed to meet for lunch at El Patio on Guadalupe.

El Patio was a true Austin icon. Founded in 1954 by a Lebanese family that still owned and operated the restaurant, El Patio quickly became a local gathering hole, a place where you could regularly spot Texas coaches and politicians, along with well-disguised musicians and other celebrities. Little had changed at El Patio over the years, with the notable exception that they now served *chips* and salsa, rather than the saltine crackers and salsa that had always been their trademark. But you could still order crackers instead of the chips, and many old-timers did, for old time's sake. El Patio originally became popular because of its prices, not the quality of its Mexican food — an old Austin joke claimed the food was Leb-Mex, not Tex-Mex — but as prices rose the locals continued to come. El Patio was a Mexican food equivalent of the old Cheers bar, a place that offered comfort and solace in the fact that nothing ever

173

changed. It was *home*. If you were a regular, you never even had to order — the waiters would just bring you your usual.

When Dave walked in, Marc had already ordered for them. A salad plate for Dave, and a #3 with extra enchilada and Perkins' taco for Marc. Marc was spooning some hot sauce onto his cracker. "Hey, Dave, I ordered you a salad plate. That okay?"

Dave slid into a chair across from his partner. "Perfect." He looked around, checking out the ancient mural on the wall beside him, then grabbed a spoon and a cracker for himself. "What's up?"

Marc pulled out a wad of papers from a satchel on the floor between his feet. "Well, Elle put together another focus group last night. Thanks to your new back end code, we were able to test out the startup sequence, where players log in to the online game."

Elle had kept Dave in the loop about the plan to test out the startup. He nodded at Marc to continue.

"The thing is, we've been running under the assumption that we could somehow balance the number of players between the two sides, NATO and opposition forces, which is critical to how the MMO functions. In fact, Sanders even challenged us on that assumption early on, and we told him that gamers would be happy playing on the Dark Side." Dave acknowledged remembering the exchange, which happened during their first meeting with the Lockheed team. Marc went on. "However, based upon the feedback we got last night, we may have been way off in our estimates of how many players would go Dark."

"How way off?" Dave asked.

"*Way* off. Completely off the charts, in fact. We tried several scenarios, basically variations on letting players pick which side they wanted, and then forcing players who chose NATO to instead fight as opposition. The results were pretty ugly."

Marc shoved a piece of paper across the table at Dave. On it was a chart summarizing the results from the various scenarios they had tested, with a summary description of each scenario spelled out at the bottom of the page. "As you can see, Dave, only about eight to ten percent consistently picked the opposition side, leaving roughly ninety percent for NATO." Dave let out a low whistle, and Marc pointed to the third column. "And here's what happened when we tried to balance the two sides by forcing some of the players who chose NATO to play instead as Russians or Chinese."

Dave snatched up the sheet of paper. "Nineteen percent? That's all?"

Marc was wearing a grim smile and shaking his head slowly. "Yeah, only nineteen percent of the players we switched wanted to continue playing the game. By the way, that's nineteen percent of the ninety percent, so it's really about seventeen percent of the total. Add in the volunteer Dark players, and that means we can only count on about twenty-five percent to play Dark."

"But that won't work!" Dave objected. "That's three to one, there's no way to make that balance out. Even if I somehow expanded the assets available to Dark players, they would get swamped by the force of numbers alone. You've got three times the number of players watching your every move, there's just no way you can react in time."

"Exactly. That's why I thought you needed to see this right away." Marc slid another sheet of paper across the table. On it was a breakdown of the demographics of the test group, along with a correlation of various demographic traits to the willingness to play for the Dark side. "One thing I checked on is whether this result is biased by the fact that Austin in general and the university in particular are so liberal. Maybe areas of the country that are more conservative might respond differently. But, as you can see, it actually works the other way. The more liberal you are, the more likely you are to go Dark. Which, of course, makes sense — conservatives are much more likely to want to fight for the good old U S of A."

"So, if anything, this pattern will be worse when we spread it out across the entire country," Dave suggested.

"Right. I mean, this is just one panel, and it's taken from just one population group, so it's possible that your results may vary. But given the enormous difference between the Dark and the Light, I don't think that will happen. Just to be sure, though, I asked Elle to put together some kind of online instrument to test gamer attitudes about their preferences for the two sides."

Dave thought about that. "How would you do that? How can you locate people to test, and then get them to do it?"

"That's exactly what I asked. But Elle came up with a brilliant idea. Remember the Kickstarter concept? She proposes we go ahead with that, and offer a free copy of the game to the first one hundred people who complete her survey. After that, she'll change the offer to a free game for the first one thousand who pony up ten bucks."

"But that's just ten thousand dollars. That won't even cover our weekly running rate at this point," Dave pointed out. "And after the cost of manufacturing and shipping the game, we're probably going to lose money on the deal."

"No, you're right, Dave, but money isn't the point. What we are really going after is early buzz. Elle has sunk a lot of thought into the idea, and last week she showed me an outline of a marketing plan that actually makes a lot of sense, part of it based on the feedback we've been getting from the focus groups. She wants to build cascading layers of awareness, of buzz, in our target market. Start with the Kickstarter campaign, where we can use the new demos you put together to get players excited about the game. Then we show them the action, the break-through level of realism that sets the game apart from anything they've ever seen before."

Marc was really starting to get excited. Their food had come, but Marc barely touched his. "Dave, these guys have been saving their pennies and nickels to buy that crappy game *Fallout*, for God's sake. Virtual reality that looks more like a Disney cartoon than anything in real life. And the rest of the Xbox games are no better. But what you've put together is a real game changer! One bite at the demo for *Dronewars* and they'll be hooked."

Dave examined the two sheets of paper in front of him again as Marc finally noticed his food and grabbed a fork to rake in a bite of cheese enchilada. While Marc was finishing his bite and chasing it down with some iced tea, Dave summarized what he had pulled from the discussion so far. "So, you're saying Kickstarter gets their attention, which then gets them to pay attention to the demo we post online. And, once they see the demo, they start to get excited, tell their friends to check it out, and people start posting online. Everything snowballs. I like it. It's definitely worth trying."

"And on top of that, Elle runs a marketing survey that confirms what we learned in the focus group," Marc added.

"In fact," Dave suggested, "we could continue market testing with the group, maybe even expand to the first thousand as well, and ship them early beta copies to get some feedback on what they like about the game play and what they don't think really works."

"That's a great idea, Dave. I'll let Elle know to build that into the Kickstarter messaging somehow. This is going to work out great!"

A cautionary flag suddenly popped up in Dave's head. "One big concern, though. So far we've been flying under the radar. If we go public with our game design at this point, won't that give away our idea to competitors? What's to stop someone from stealing our idea and beating us to the punch?"

"Who could beat us, Dave? We already have a huge head start, plus we have exclusive access to the flight sim code and all the CAD designs from the DOD. The only company that could have any

178

chance at all of beating us to market is Dovetail, and they signed a nondisclosure and non-compete with us. So even if they tried, we'd own their ass in court. And, of course, there is no real way they could pull it off, anyway, without Microsoft knowing about it and giving us the high sign, which they haven't."

"Yeah, you're right, Marc. Okay, I'm all in. Let's go for it." Dave motioned to his plate. "Meanwhile, this isn't getting any warmer."

"Good point," Marc noted, finally digging into his meal with gusto. "I'll touch base with Elle on this after lunch. She suggested this morning she might be able to turn this around quickly. Maybe even by this weekend."

"Meanwhile," Dave added, "we need to assume that the feedback we got was valid, so I need to start noodling on how in the world I can fix it." He finished his lunch quietly, already absorbed with ideas on how to rebalance forces on the two sides of the game.

36

On Wednesday, Julia and Elle took off for Fashion Week in Dallas. Elle had launched the Kickstarter campaign on Monday morning, and it was completely subscribed by Monday evening. She was swamped the rest of the week as her MBA teams completed projects in time for spring break, so she had little time to pour over the survey results before jumping into Julia's red Miata for the trip north.

"I can put the top up if you need it," Julia suggested. "But it's such a pretty day, and the drive really sucks, so I thought it might be nice to go topless."

"No, that's great. A little sun on our faces and wind through our hair would be nice, particularly since I've spent the past week stuck inside the B-school with my head buried in the books." Elle did pull out a baseball cap to shield her face from the sun, and decided not to worry about the survey results until later, when they were both settled into the hotel. They were a little late getting out of Austin, so the drive north through Round Rock would be stop and go, and the rest of the way into Dallas was almost completely under construction. Elle thought Julia could use a little distraction from the headaches of driving. "By the way, Jules, where did you put all your stuff for the booth? There's no way any of it is in this car. We barely had room for our bags."

Julia shot her a quick smile. "I shipped all of that out last week, and it's being assembled as we speak. We just need to swing by early in the morning to make sure everything is ready and in place before the hall opens at noon. Surely you didn't think I was going to risk these nails with all those boxes and poles?" Julia held up her right hand, showing off her blood-red fingernails, almost an exact match for the car.

"Oh my gosh, no!" Elle laughed. "What was I thinking?" She dug into her purse for her phone. "If you don't mind, I put together a little playlist for the trip. We won't get anything on the radio once we leave Georgetown and until we get almost to Dallas. That okay?"

"That's perfect! Thanks! If we just had a bottle of wine this trip would go by swimmingly." Julia swung out onto Mopac Expressway, which was already a parking lot. The drive north was slow but uneventful, and it was already dark by the time the girls pulled into the Hyatt. Elle grabbed their bags from the boot while Julia tossed her keys to the valet.

Too tired from the trip to bother with the restaurant, they settled into the room and ordered room service. Julia was just about to order a bottle of wine when Elle pulled a 1.5 liter bottle of Clos du Bois Chardonnay from her suitcase. "Well, you said a bottle of wine would go swimmingly. And if we're going to swim in wine tonight, we should definitely make sure it's a big pool."

"I like how you roll, Elle," Julia replied, quickly completing their order. "Do I need to ask them to—" She paused as Elle pulled out a wine opener and waved it around in triumph. "No, I see you've got that covered, too."

181

The two girls were already into their second glass each by the time the food arrived. Julia signed off on the bill and a generous tip, and they set the cart between the two queen-sized beds and started in on the feast.

In between bites and emboldened by the wine, Elle decided to pry a bit into Julia's personal life. "I know you're originally from somewhere in northern California. Is that where your family's from?"

"Well, yes, sort of." Julia seemed reluctant at first to open up, but finally decided to just let go. The wine was talking to her, and she knew she really needed to start developing some lasting friendships in Austin if she was going to be stuck down there for a while.

"So do you still have family back there?" Elle continued.

"Not much family anymore. Just one grandmother."

"So where are your parents if I might ask? They're not divorced, are they?"

"No. Not divorced—" A pained look flashed across Julia's eyes.

"Oh! I'm sorry if I stepped into something!" Elle's cheeks had flushed bright red. "Look, we should talk about something else—"

"No, that's okay," Julia replied. "It's just not something I think about very much. It's a bit complicated, and it all happened so very long ago. But I guess it's a good thing to talk about it every now and then. To be honest, even Dave hasn't heard the whole story."

182

"Here, at least let me top you off," Elle offered, filling Julia's glass almost to the brim.

"Thanks." Julia took a sip of the wine. "Where to begin?" She paused again, gazing deeply into her glass, as if she was looking back at pictures from the past. "I was almost two years old at the time. We lived in Malibu, a few blocks from where my mom grew up. Her parents still lived in the old house, very close to the shops. Mom and Dad were at a party at the Getty Villa, some big high society thing, and had left me with my grandparents. 1 was their first and only child, and they still didn't trust me with babysitters, I suppose. Money, of course, wasn't ever an issue. Anyway, it was late, and they were driving back to Malibu on the Pacific Coast Highway. There was a slight bend in the road, right around Carbon Canyon."

Julia looked up at Elle. "I was very young, you know, so I don't have any actual memory of any of this. And my family never ever talked about it. I guess it was all just too painful for them. So really, all I know was what was reported in the papers at the time. I looked up the articles a few years ago. I guess I was just looking for a little closure."

"Julia, we don't have to—" Elle began.

"No, that's all right. As I said, it's probably good to share it every now and then." Julia took another sip of wine, and Elle noticed that her chin was beginning to quiver ever so slightly. "The police think it was a drunk driver. Crossed over the median toward my parents. But they don't know, and they never identified anyone responsible. All they know is what they learned from the tire marks. At some point my parents' car turned abruptly to the left. There was evidently some effort to straighten out and get back on the road, but it was too late. The car plunged through the guard rail and flew over the cliff."

"Julia, I'm so sorry—" Elle was in tears, and Julia could no longer hold back, either. In between soft sobs, Julia finished her story.

"They didn't find them until hours later. My grandmother got concerned when it got late and they still weren't home, so she called the police. The California Highway Patrol found them. The report in the paper said they died instantly, but then that's just something they say to make it less painful for the family. They probably laid there bleeding out for some time before they finally died."

"So what happened to you?" Elle asked tearfully.

"I stayed with my mother's family for a few years, but then my grandfather died of cancer, and my grandmother joined him not long after, I think from a broken heart. Just too much loss in her life too soon. I then moved out to Oxnard, where my dad's family lived. My last grandfather died while I was in high school. My grandmother is in an Alzheimer's home there."

"So you don't have anyone left?"

"I have a couple of uncles and their families, but not anyone close. And, having to change schools just before high school, I never really developed any lifelong childhood friends. So for the most part it's just been me all of my life."

"That is so sad, Julia!" Elle had moved around the food cart to sit beside Julia, holding her hands.

"I think the worst part is I never got to know my parents. Especially my mother, who was apparently a very successful surgeon. I tried a few times to get my grandparents to talk about them, but I don't think they had the strength to dredge up all the old feelings."

Julia picked up a pillow to dab at her eyes. "But it's not all bad. It could be worse. I mean, I knew girls who had it *really* bad at home, whose parents were monsters. My grandparents were very good to me. A little old, and way out of touch, but still very kind, very loving souls."

"So, are you getting over all that now?" Elle asked.

"There's not really much to get over, Elle, other than I learned to be pretty resilient, and to put up walls. I think I was afraid to get close to people, afraid I would get left behind again. That was really bad when my first set of grandparents died, and I had to move to Oxnard. In fact, that was probably one of the reasons I agreed to move to Austin with Dave. He was one of the only guys I've dated in many years — actually, since high school — who wasn't just a complete jerk. Guys who didn't give a damn about me, but just wanted to try to get into my panties."

The bottle was almost empty, and the wine was having a strong impact on the two women.

"When Dave asked me to move, at first I thought *no way*. I mean, you know Austin. It's nice for Texas, but compared to San

Francisco it's a cultural wasteland." Elle, her words becoming a little slurred, couldn't help but agree. To girls raised in the Bay Area, *everywhere* else was a cultural wasteland. "But then he came up with that crazy plan to open up a dress shop for me. To be honest, it wasn't really anything I was all that excited about, but he insisted on doing it. And that's why we're here tonight."

Elle was surprised. "You didn't want to open up the shop? Then why did you agree to do it?"

"Because it was absolutely the sweetest thing anyone had ever done for me. I mean, I know he was trying to bribe me into moving east, and he needed something to keep me busy while he was working on the game. But really, at the heart of it, he was just trying to make me happy. And he worked so hard to make it all seem like an investment, just an ordinary business deal, so I wouldn't think he was trying to buy me. The truth is, if he *was* just trying to buy me, he wouldn't be there in the store so much helping me out. He wouldn't have cancelled his plans for this week to be here for me. You just don't have to dig very deep into Dave's heart to see how devoted he is to me."

Elle was confused. "But if you don't really want to do this, why are you working so hard at it?"

"Well, I wasn't really sure at first. If you can keep a secret, I am *not* one of those girls who really gets off on shopping. And I can give or take a nice pair of heels. But, unlike all the other men I've dated, Dave cares about me more than just what I look like. More than just what I can give him in bed. He is truly an amazing man."

186

Elle jumped on that tidbit. "Amazing, eh? Time to dish!"

"No, not that!" Julia blushed deeply. "Amazing as a *person*. Not to say I have any complaints in the other department, by the way. But what I mean is that Dave is the kindest, sweetest, the *smartest* person I have ever known. And he loves me, more than anyone else has ever loved me. And so I wanted to show him how much I appreciated that love. I want him to be as amazed by me as I am by him. The *inside* me, not the me that still thinks she's that frumpy little fat girl from junior high."

"I can't believe you were ever fat."

"Yes, girlfriend, it's true. And in my head I still am. And that isn't all bad. It helps keep me motivated to pass on that last bite of pasta, or—" pointing to the empty wine bottle, "just say *no* when friends try to get me to pour down empty calories that get me saying stupid things! Speaking of which, now it's *your* turn to dish."

"Oh, Julia, I'd love to, but I am way too dizzy from all that wine to get started tonight. I might accidentally let slip about some of Marc's own... unique talents. I think we should just take a rain check on this discussion until later."

"Unique, eh? Now you've got *me* interested. Okay, then, a rain check for now, but you better be ready with the *whole* story next time. And I'm talking actual *dimensions!*"

The two of them were still giggling when they pulled back the covers and turned out the lights.

37

ave was starting to regret agreeing to come with Marc to the SXSW Gaming Expo. After swinging by the Geek Stage and the Indie Corner, they strolled past the almost 200 booths at the expo. Everyone was showing off their new or reworked games, and since the expo was open for free to the general public, the place was packed.

Marc, of course, was in his element, using his phone's camera to sneak shots of various booths and exhibitors, and already making plans for their own booth at next year's expo. Marc was also much better at schmoozing with people he'd never met before, exchanging contact info with the other marketing types. At the end of the day, to game industry professionals these events were more about networking than anything else, and networking paid off big time when you needed an answer really fast or needed feedback on a potential vendor.

But Dave had real work to do, and the carnival atmosphere held no appeal for him. He quickly decided to skip out early and see if Jack Travers was available for a mid-afternoon flight to Dallas Love Field. He had originally planned to come back on Friday for another day at the expo, but one hour in, he had already seen more than enough. He'd just take his computer and work in the hotel room while Jules worked the fashion booth downstairs.

38

Dave caught Travers on his cell phone just as the pilot was refueling his plane for a flight back to Austin from College Station. Travers suggested they could save some time by meeting at the Georgetown airport, just a short thirty minute drive north, rather than have both of them fight their way through traffic to the Lakeway Airport southwest of Austin, Dave on the ground and Travers through the crowded Austin airspace. Dave could stash his car at Georgetown Muny for free, and the flight up to Dallas would take just a little over an hour.

Georgetown Municipal Airport was tucked off the main highway, on the north side of Georgetown just west of Interstate 35. Dave relied on the navigation system in his Honda HR-V to tell him when and where to turn, and soon he was pulling up to the small terminal building, located right across the parking lot from the airport's tower. The terminal was one of the last surviving examples of the old Magnolia Oil facilities that were constructed in the 1940's to sell oil and aviation gas to general aviation pilots. It was renovated and expanded in 2002, and still retained the quaint charm of its past, including a red metal phone booth standing next to the tarmac.

Dave parked right in front of the terminal, grabbed his bags and headed inside. Jack Travers was already sitting in the conference room, pouring over navigation maps. Although aviation maps were now freely available on tablets and computers, Travers preferred to spread out the old-fashioned paper maps as he plotted his flights.

"Dave!" Travers exclaimed, giving Dave's hand a firm shake. "Come take a look-see—"

Travers spun the map around as Dave grabbed a seat at the table. "Just wanted to show you where we're headed today." He pointed to a spot on the map just above Austin. "This is where we are right now, that spot that says GTU. That's the airport designator for Georgetown Municipal Airport. This line here," he indicated a mostly straight line just east of GTU and running roughly north and south, "is I-35. We'll largely be following that as we head into Dallas. Normally I'd deviate a bit and buzz some of the lakes and other scenery, to give you a bird's eye view, as it were, but today we'll be flying IFR, so we have to stay pretty much on course the whole way." Dave knew from his flight sim work that IFR meant Instrument Flight Rules. Pilots flying IFR had to file an official flight plan with air traffic control, and then had to follow that plan exactly unless a serious problem developed demanding a deviation from that course.

"Why wouldn't we just go VFR?" Dave asked. Visual Flight Rules didn't require a flight plan, giving pilots more freedom on where and when to fly.

"Normally I would, but Love Field is inside the DFW Class Bravo airspace, so we need clearance to approach and land. We could pick up that clearance in the air as we got close, but since we're already so close to the outer edges of that space, we might as well get that lined up in advance while we're still on the ground. Coming back, though, we won't have that problem, so if the weather stays clear we can do some sightseeing then."

Dave was really looking forward to this flight. Even though very few of the actual details of general aviation translated into the *Dronewars* game, Dave had spent a great deal of time flying GA aircraft in the Prepar3D software as he tested early modifications of the demo, and in the process he had gotten a little hooked on flying. Maybe, if the game really took off and they made a pile of money, he might take some lessons and learn to fly the real thing.

Travers folded up the map and they headed outside. His Piper PA-28 Cherokee was parked on the tarmac just past the gas pumps. The plane was mostly white, with a burgundy belly and matching burgundy stripes on top of the wheel fairings. Travers opened the passenger side door for Dave. "Just toss your bags in the back seat," he instructed, walking back behind the aircraft and around to the pilot's side.

"Don't we need to weigh these or something?" Dave asked.

"No, we're okay. Technically, you're supposed to do what we call a weight and balance calculation to make sure we're not overweight, or tail-heavy or nose-heavy. But after you've flown for a while you get a feel for whether that's going to be a problem or not. As it is, I probably already burned off more fuel just flying over from Aggieland than your suitcase weighs, and at any rate we're still a couple hundred pounds on the light side of any trouble."

Dave stepped up on the wing, pushed his suitcase and computer into the back, and climbed into his seat. The Cherokee was equipped with dual controls, so just in front of Dave was a control yoke, and when he stretched out, his feet rested on rudder pedals. He self-consciously shrunk back, not wanting to have anything to do with causing the plane to go out of control and crash.

Travers finished some last-minute checks and climbed into the pilot seat, shutting and locking the door and reaching over to make sure Dave's door was locked, as well. He turned the key in the ignition and the engine started right up, the instruments on the dash in front of them immediately springing to life.

"Hey, Jack." Dave pointed to the old-fashioned looking instruments that covered most of the dash. "The Cessna I flew in the flight simulator had a big computer screen in the middle and very few of these instruments, but it looks here like you have just the opposite, a small GPS and a ton of dedicated gauges."

"Yeah, I would love to spend the money to get a glass panel setup, but this Piper just can't support the cost. A really decent setup would cost almost as much as I spent on the plane itself."

"But isn't it safer?"

"Maybe. Maybe not. It helps a bit with situational awareness, having a good mental image of where you are at all moments, but some people think all the full-screen doodads just make pilots lazy, and they wind up staring at the screen in flight instead of keeping their eyes focused outside the plane. Which is really where they should be most of the time. As it is, I've got this little black-and-white GPS on the panel that certifies me for point-to-point navigation, so I don't have to always track the VORs when I'm IFR. Plus, I've got this portable unit here." Travers pointed to the color GPS attached to his flight yoke. "It isn't certified but it still gives me almost everything else I need. And if my primary flight instruments go haywire, which they did once about a year back, I can press a button on the portable and get a virtual six-pack of instruments that will get me safely back on the ground." He pushed a button, and the GPS map changed to show replicas of an airspeed indicator, attitude indicator, altimeter, vertical speed indicator, heading indicator and turn coordinator. He switched it back to map view.

"Well, we're burning avgas, my friend, so let's get this show on the road." Travers radioed the tower for clearance to taxi to Runway 18, the airport's primary runway. "Tower, this is Piper Four Zero Papa at Terminal, request taxi to runway1-8." The tower controller immediately radioed back, "Four Zero Papa, taxi to runway 1-8."

Travers released the hand brake, eased the power up slightly, and slowly steered the plane to the right using the rudder pedals. He turned right again at the taxiway, finally pulling the plane to a complete stop in a holding area short of the runway.

"Why are we stopping?" Dave asked over the internal intercom.

"Got to do some last minute checks and get final clearance." Travers engaged the hand brake again and revved the engine, switching the ignition key back and forth to check the magnetos. He keyed the radio to check for final IFR clearance, then nodded to Dave. "Tower, Four Zero Papa ready at runway 1-8 for northbound IFR departure." "Four Zero Papa, cleared for departure runway 1-8. On crosswind contact Departure Control One-One-Niner-Point-Zero," the tower radioed back. " One-One-Niner-Point-Zero," Travers repeated.

Travers eased the throttle forward again, turning the plane right and then left onto the runway. Without pausing, he straightened the plane and applied full throttle. The little plane quickly gathered speed, and at 55 knots he pulled back on the yoke and the Cherokee was airborne. Travers had entered the frequency for Austin Departure Control into his second radio prior to leaving the ground, and as he banked the plane to the left he flipped the switch for the second radio. "Departure, this is Piper One Six Three Four Zero Papa, out of Georgetown for Dallas Love Field."

"Four Zero Papa, squawk 1127 and identify."

Travers dialed in 1127 on his transponder and pushed the identifier button, causing his plane's location to flash briefly on the air traffic controller's radar screen. "Four Zero Papa, we have you on radar. Climb to ten thousand and continue direct to Love Field."

"Ten thousand, direct Love Field," Travers answered. He adjusted his course and altitude on the autopilot, then released the yoke and settled back.

"Now we just sit back and enjoy the ride, Dave." Travers was joking, of course. For the next hour he stayed busy confirming his course bearings and responding to radio calls from ATC as he was repeatedly handed off from one controller to another. Dave, however, did sit back to enjoy the trip. The sky was deep blue, except for some light cirrus well above the aircraft and an occasional small cloud that they burst through like it was cotton candy. Dave's view of the ground was somewhat limited because of the low-wing design of the Cherokee, but it was infinitely better than the view he was used to getting in commercial aircraft, peering through a small window cut into the side of a passenger jet.

Travers kept Dave entertained throughout the flight by explaining the functionality of the various instruments, particularly the navigation gauges that Dave had seen on the panels of his flight sim aircraft but had never really understood. Finally, Travers was instructed to switch over to Love Field tower, who vectored him to intercept the instrument landing system beacon north of runway 13L. Air traffic control had left them a little too high for the Dallas approach, unfortunately, so Travers tapped on an instrument he called the HSI and informed Dave that he was in for a treat.

"We need to drop about two thousand feet pretty quickly to get on the vertical landing slope. You can see here that we are way too high." Travers pointed to yellow tick marks on either side of the HSI. "The solid yellow marker is our glide slope. As you can see, it is way beneath us, so we need to 'fly down' to meet it. That gets us in the right vertical position to land. The problem is, if I just push in on the yoke and point the plane down, we'll pick up a lot of speed and we won't have any way of dumping that speed off before landing.

"Luckily, there's a good alternative, and one that I bet you've never heard of, because it's not a maneuver that is practical in commercial passenger planes. We're going to try a forward slip, where I'll turn the yoke to bank the plane to the left, all while applying opposite rudder. To you, it will look like we're trying to fly away from the airport, but watch, and you'll see that the plane will continue to move straight toward the runway. The key, here, is that it reduces the lift on the wings, because the air is forced to move along the wings, rather than across them, and that makes us drop like a rock." Travers immediately turned the yoke, and the plane seemed to spin to the left. Dave felt the resulting drop in his stomach as the plane quickly lost altitude, but sure enough the plane seemed to remain straight on course for the runway he could see out the right side.

In just about a minute, Travers eased the yoke back to the right, straightening the aircraft with its nose pointing directly down the runway. Dave glanced at the HSI and saw that the glide slope marker was dead on center, as was the vertical line that Travers had called the lubber line, indicating the center of the runway. Travers eased back a little more on the power, and the number 13L painted on the end of the runway quickly expanded as the airplane shot for the runway. It seemed at first like the plane was going to land short of the runway, but Travers pulled back on the yoke and the Cherokee's nose rose in a gentle flare. Their descent rate trailed off, and the plane touched down softly on the runway just past the numbers. Travers taxied the plane to Signature Flight Support, one of many fixed base operators located on the airport that provided refueling and other services to general aviation customers. "Landmark generally has better fuel prices, but you can usually count on Signature to have a free crew car available, so you don't have to rent a car if you want to run around Dallas for a few hours," Travers explained.

"They let you have a free loaner car?" Dave asked.

"Well, it isn't exactly free, because they count on you buying avgas to make up for it. And with avgas selling on the north side of eight bucks a gallon here, that quickly adds up to big gas bill. So the crew car is a perk that brings them customers that might otherwise swing over to Landmark to save a buck a gallon." Travers pulled the plane into to an open parking space with a practiced ease, killing the engine and jumping out to secure the tie-downs as Dave gathered his belongings from the back seat. "You want a ride over to the hotel? I'm headed in that direction, and it wouldn't be a problem."

"Hey, thanks, Jack, that would be great." Dave hoisted his overnight onto his left shoulder, grabbing the computer bag with his right. "Jules won't be done with the booth for another hour or so, so I was just planning on cooling my heels here and waiting for her. But if you're headed that way anyway, I'd really appreciate the lift."

The two dropped off the keys to the airplane at the front desk, with Travers signing a fuel order and retrieving the keys to a crew car parked out front. In minutes they were on their way to the hotel. "Wow, Jack, that is amazingly convenient." Dave gushed. "No security to deal with, no lines, just in and out in a heartbeat."

"Welcome to the joys of general aviation, Dave." Travers was already climbing into the driver's seat of the loaner. "It may be expensive as hell, but in the end it's the only way to fly."

Dave heartily agreed with that notion, and once again made a silent promise to take up flying himself, assuming *Dronewars* took off. He chuckled at the unintentional pun, and began to think about all of the small things he had learned on the short flight that he needed to incorporate into the game action. Just the forward slip maneuver alone would be a heck of a trick to pull during combat, but without rudder pedals for the Xbox he would need to figure out how to combine a button press with the joystick controls to simulate the cross-control inputs. *Flight Simulator* usually bypassed rudder controls to make flying easier for new gamers, but Dave knew that rudder control could be switched on in the game for more advanced simulations. *What if I give the player an option to switch to advanced mode, then use the left joystick for banking into turns and the right joystick for rudder control? Assuming he could master the use of the rudders, that would actually give a pilot much better control over the simulated plane.* Dave was so engrossed in the list of changes he wanted to make that he was surprised when they finally pulled up in front of the hotel.

"Sure you don't want a ride home tomorrow morning?" Travers asked as Dave collected his bags from the rear seat.

"Nah, the gaming panels are a total bore. I'll let Marc handle that, and I'll just get some work done in the hotel. I'll see you Sunday afternoon, though, if you're still on. And how much do I owe you for the gas?"

Travers waved him off. "Fuhgettaboutit! Anytime I can take a virgin on his first plane ride, it's more than worth it," Travers explained with a sly wink. "And besides, speaking of virgins, I managed to line up a date for tonight with a hottie I met in a bar last month on my last trip through here."

"Ah," Dave laughed. "So instead of a different girl in every port, for you it's a different girl in every *air*port."

"Something like that. You ought to try it, Dave. Variety is the spice of life."

"Thanks, but having just one woman in my life keeps me busy enough. Plus, you know Jules. She's way out of my league. No way I could ever get that lucky again."

"Well, if things ever change, give me a call and I'll be happy to fix you up. See you on Sunday, Dave."

"See ya, buddy. And thanks again!" Dave gathered his bags and headed into the hotel.

39

The Hyatt hotel was located in downtown Dallas, so after the fashion exhibits closed, Jules and Elle changed into jeans and blouses and they all headed out to the historic West End for dinner. The West End first became famous as the location for President John Kennedy's assassination, and a museum had since been established in the former Texas Schoolbook Depository building where Lee Harvey Oswald fired his fatal shots. Development of the West End as an evening destination spot in the mid-1970's had been vital to the resurgence of Dallas' downtown, and although the area had seen a slow decline in recent years, it still remained one of Dallas' premiere tourist attractions.

Compared to Austin, the restaurant scene in the West End was somewhat forgettable, mostly national chains catering to comfort food. But Julia was too tired from working the booth all day to try anything upscale, so they settled on RJ's Mexican Cuisine. Dave ordered three Mexican martinis and a bowl of dirty queso to start, and they decided to split a large order of fajitas in order to leave room later for cookies at Tiff's Treats.

The show was going amazingly well. Julia's designs were selling quickly, especially the new collection of *Jules' Jewels*, and several major fashion outlets had already shown an interest in carrying her line. She had even been approached by a potential investor who wanted to talk further about taking the store nationwide. Dave just sat back throughout dinner and listened to her jabbering excitedly about all the people she had met and all the possibilities for the future. The little shop he had helped create just to lure her to Austin looked like it might actually be taking off, and Dave gazed across the table at his beautiful and talented girlfriend and wondered once again how he had ever gotten so lucky.

Elle was also deeply engaged in the conversation, throwing in various ideas for managing the *Jules* brand and suggesting a potential strategy of forcing an artificial scarcity of product in order to built the illusion of exclusivity. "You can either be a Chevy or a Cadillac," she explained. "At their heart, they are 95% the same car, but one sells for several times the price of the other. Why? Because a huge segment of the market is driven by self image, not by the value proposition. Sure, you can sell a greater volume of clothing in a Walmart or Target, but you can realize a bigger profit in the end by sticking to Neiman's or Nordy's. Especially when it comes to fashion, where it is *all* about image."

Dave understood the concept, but as an official software god he generally left marketing and positioning to Marc. Or, increasingly, to Elle, who had taken a much greater interest in *Dronewars* as they inched closer to launch, and was already making a huge impact on their own launch plans and marketing. *I guess with Marc and Elle I wound up with two for the price of one*, Dave thought. And, judging from the way Elle was engaging with Julia on marketing plans for her fashion line, maybe the partnership would wind up even more lucrative than that.

201

40

After breakfast in the hotel restaurant the next morning, the girls headed back to the convention center and Dave set up shop with his laptop at the small desk in their hotel room. He started the day by typing up a long list of ideas that had come to him during the afternoon flight up to Dallas, using an Excel spreadsheet to organize general ideas on the left with implementation details fleshed out on the right. He was just finishing up the list when his cell phone rang. He glanced down and didn't recognize the number, a 202 area code. Normally he let unknown numbers roll over to voice mail, but with everything heating up toward launch, he decided to take the call, anyway.

"Dave Elliott here," he answered. "How can I help you?"

"Dave, glad I caught you! This is Bob Sanders."

Strange. Sanders always works through Marc, Dave wondered, caught completely off guard. "Great to hear from you, Bob," Dave replied. "To what do I owe this honor?"

"Ha! No honor, Dave. I just had some things come up that I thought I might swing past you, if you've got the time."

"Sure, no problem. I'm just working on some small adjustments to the game controls for the drones and small aircraft. How can I help you?" Dave was wary of Sanders, but tried not to let it show. Sanders never called without wanting something. Just what exactly was he up to this morning?

"I was actually hoping maybe I could help you," Sanders explained. "I had a meeting with Carla and some of the guys running the DOD database, where we get the models for the various aircraft, boats and weapons. They tell me they've been playing with the latest cut of your software and comparing the simulation of various objects to how they actually perform in real life. They all said you've done a really terrific job, and they're very impressed, by the way, but they had some ideas on how you could improve the realism a bit."

"Well, I'm always up for that, Bob," Dave agreed. "What do they have in mind?"

"My understanding is that they've monkeyed with the database settings, things like acceleration, drag, all that, and they were able to adjust some of the entries to make the realism almost dead-on perfect. I wondered if you might want them to shoot you a copy to take a gander at. Get your opinion on whether they're on the money on any of this."

Dave thought about what Sanders had just told him. Changes to the avatar database should have zero impact on his code, and he could try out all the changes before committing them to the final database, so there was no real downside risk and a lot to be gained in terms of realism. For free. "That sounds like a great idea, Bob. Thanks! Any help I can get making this game as close to real life as possible is always appreciated. Just have them ship me a copy of the entries and I'll test them out and slip them in."

"That'll be great, Dave. That gets them a little closer to having the simulation working spot on for when we finally get the war games software running, so they're happy being able to get a jump on things to speed that up. Oh, and one other small thing."

Here it goes, Dave thought. *The other shoe drops*. "Okay, what is it?"

"Well, it seems they have some, how shall we say it, experimental weapons and drones that they've modeled that they'd like to play with in your software, to give some feedback to the folks building the new toys on how they perform and what tweaks to be mindful of down the road. If you don't have an objection, they'd like to stick those in your pre-launch database just for testing. Carla will make sure they're pulled out before launch, of course. We can't actually have models of our experimental equipment sitting out in the open on all those game consoles, can we?" Sanders chuckled.

"But why do we need it in our database?" Dave wondered. "Why can't they try it out on their copies of the game the same way they did the improved avatar models they're sending me?"

"I don't know for sure, Dave," Sanders explained. "Something about having to make changes every time you tweak the code or database. It's not critical, they can work around it. They just thought that might make their job a little easier."

"Okay, sure, I don't have a problem with that, as long as Carla takes responsibility for putting them into the database and pulling them out. But, by the way, she could have done that without me even knowing, because the database is really her responsibility. So you didn't actually need to ask my permission."

"No, but I just didn't want you poking around and accidentally stumbling onto the new entries without my asking you first." Sanders paused. "That's our policy, you know. Complete transparency, no surprises. That always works better for the relationship."

"Right, no surprises," Dave agreed. "Well, thanks for the heads up, and for all the work your guys have done on our avatar models. I'm looking forward to seeing the changes they've made. And, by the way, please pass my appreciation on to your guys."

"I'll do that. And I know that, as much as they are doing this to get a head start on the war games software, they're also jazzed about getting to be a part of building an Xbox game. They're all geeks, after all, just like you guys, so working with you fellows is a big thrill for them."

Dave had never considered that. "Yeah, the only thing that is more fun than playing the game is actually creating the game. Programming is the ultimate video game."

"I'll just take your word on that, Dave. I can barely work my damn phone. And speaking of which, I have another call coming in, so I'll have to go. I'll get the guys to send that stuff to you ASAP."

"That'd be great. Thanks, Bob." The call ended, and Dave went back to his spreadsheet. *I can't wait to see if some of the adjustments they made map into the ideas I got out of my flight yesterday. It is really interesting how differently things can appear on paper versus how they behave in real life.*

41

arc drove up early Friday evening, eagerly anticipating their planned double date out on the town in Dallas. But the girls' excitement from the evening before had devolved into utter exhaustion, so eventually they all decided to just order in pizza to go along with several bottles of wine Marc had brought up with him from Austin. Dave checked Google for recommendations, and decided to try Olivella's, named one of the best pizzerias in the country by USA Today. Since Marc had already suffered through the long drive up from Austin fighting heavy construction, Dave volunteered to run out and pick up the pizza, grabbing Marc's keys to his Lexus for the trip.

The heavy pizza and a bottle of wine apiece soon took their toll, and Dave and Julia said their goodbyes early and headed off to bed. They all agreed to meet up first thing the next morning, however, and venture back over to the West End for breakfast at Ellen's Southern Kitchen, a far better choice than the expensive and forgettable breakfasts served up in the Hyatt's restaurant.

After breakfast, the girls returned to the exhibit hall while Marc and Dave borrowed Julia's Miata to take a top-down tour of Dallas. Being from California, they had never spent any time in Dallas outside of the DFW airport, and since the day had turned warm and sunny, they decided to take advantage of the weather and explore.

Big D was better known for its shopping than for its tourist spots, however, and neither Marc nor Dave was particularly interested in the former, so after a short drive out to Arlington to check out Jerry's World (including a self-guided tour that set them each back almost twenty dollars), they headed back to the hotel and opted to spend the rest of the day walking around downtown. They visited the Sixth Floor Museum at Dealey Plaza and the Perot Museum of Nature and Science, then wound up at Klyde Warren Park, a five acre oasis perched atop a sunken freeway, where they enjoyed the sights and sounds of children playing and, more interestingly, a group of especially well-endowed women contorting into a variety of somewhat revealing yoga positions. For lunch they decided to try out Pecan Lodge in Deep Ellum for brisket and an assortment of sides.

The walk back to the hotel gave them a welcome opportunity to burn off the heavy barbeque that had settled into their stomachs, not to mention the buzz from a couple of draft IPAs. Marc took the opportunity to catch Dave up on what had happened at SXSW, which wasn't much, and Dave relayed the details of his discussion with Sanders the day before.

"That sounds great, Dave!" Marc exclaimed, pausing to wait for a pedestrian light to change. "Looks like a real win-win. They get a good lead on the *Warg* implementation, and you get lots of free help in fleshing out all the weaponry in the game. We're really moving ahead at light speed lately."

"Actually, we are way ahead of schedule in terms of my side of the project," Dave agreed. "I have some fine tuning to do, and I'm still playing around with optimizing how the controls work and how to use various button combos, particularly switching between the different visual perspectives for each weapon, but everything is really jelling right now. And, of course, we have that big-picture problem of figuring out how to balance the number of Dark Side players. But the big black hole right now is on the back end side. Those guys are not yet up to speed, and we have a lot of work to do with logging in users, assigning them to the various scenarios, and then getting the real-time synchronization working without any hiccups."

"Do you need more resources?" Marc suggested. "I can talk to Sanders about it if you think more warm bodies will help."

"No, I think more bodies might just have them all stumbling over one another at this point. We just need to get them fully on board, working through the project timelines. And the frustrating thing is, I am so out of my league on that side of the game that I can't really offer much in the way of help. By the time I could get comfortable with the back end code we would already be at our target launch date. So all I can do is just feed them some general ideas, and then sit back and watch."

Marc made a note to talk to Carla about moving faster on the back end development.

42

That night the four of them finally broke free for their double date, starting with a romantic dinner at The French Room, once described by the New York Times as "a Louis XV fantasy on the prairie, indisputably the most striking and sumptuous restaurant in Dallas." Since the restaurant was located in the Adolphus Hotel six or seven blocks from the Hyatt, the guys took one look at their dates' dresses and footwear and decided to spring for a cab ride to the restaurant. Hours later they all stumbled out of another cab and back into the Hyatt lobby, happy and pleasantly drunk.

The convention was over, but the four of them had already decided to stay over the extra night to celebrate and to take a well-needed break from work, particularly given the fact that the *Dronewars* launch was now just a few months away. This might be one of their last chances before then to just break loose.

Since Julia had her Miata in Dallas and Marc had driven his Lexus up, Dave no longer needed a plane ride back. He had called Travers early on Saturday morning to let him know about the change in plans. Travers sounded a bit disappointed, but they agreed to try a scenic flight around Central Texas sometime in the near future, possibly with Julia in tow.

They all slept in late the next morning, then caught brunch downstairs in the hotel restaurant and headed back to Austin.

"Davy, thank you *so* much for coming up here with me," Julia purred. "I know it wasn't much fun for you, particularly sitting around in the hotel all day Friday, but having you here made it all that much more special for me."

"Well," Dave responded with a grin, "based on last night alone, I think I would have gladly *walked* up to Dallas to spend the night with you."

"You act like you're missing out at home," Julia answered, pouting playfully. "You just need to spend less time surfing porn on your computer, or whatever it is you're doing, and more time in the bedroom with me."

"I'll assure you, Jules, if it was porn versus you, I would sell my computer tomorrow." Dave reached over to rub her thigh playfully. "Although," he continued thoughtfully, "speaking of porn, I've been thinking that *Dronewars* may be a little too much like faking it." He explained to her his insights on how airplanes really move in the air that he had gained from the short flight up to Dallas. "I think I've been approaching the sim a little too scientifically, and not really doing a good job modeling the feel of it. Kind of like focusing on individual sounds, but not paying attention to the fact that they're arranged into some form of music. If I can manage to create that *feeling* of flying in the game, it's going to make all the difference in how players respond to it, to their ultimate enjoyment of *Dronewars*."

"Hmph!" Julia responded. "That just sounds like a lot more nights with me left all alone in bed."

210

Dave looked over at her with a bit of alarm, but then he noticed the twinkle she couldn't hide in her eyes and the slow smile sneaking across her lips. "Tell you what, Jules. Why don't we plan on my being there every night when you go to bed. And after I've worn you out and you've passed out from sheer physical exhaustion, I can sneak back to my laptop for a few more hours of work—"

Julia punched him hard in the arm, smiling. "Promises, promises. If anyone's going to pass out from exhaustion, it won't be me."

"Okay, then, it's a contest." Dave rubbed at his arm with a feigned grimace. "Last one to bed tonight is a rotten egg!"

43

The database revisions from the guys at DOD arrived early Monday morning, and Dave quickly set to work testing them. He was surprised at the sheer number of revisions — it looked like DOD had modified virtually every avatar in the database. *I can't imagine how much work went into that,* Dave observed. The commitment from DOD and Lockheed appeared to be far larger than he had originally thought. Just testing the revisions to make sure they didn't corrupt the system took most of the day, but he wound up flagging only three files to send back for confirmation that they had been modified correctly.

Meanwhile, Marc sat down with Carla to discuss the problems with the back end software. "Dave thinks the logjam for launch will be on your side of the program, and he feels pretty impotent in not being able to do anything more to move it along."

"I hear you, Marc, but that's not going to be a problem. In fact, Sanders is pushing me to accelerate our possible launch date. Thought I might give you a heads up on that."

"*Accelerate* it!" Marc was flabbergasted. "Hell, we've already moved it up several months as it is! How in the world can we complete our development timelines, plus manufacturing and marketing, in any less time?"

"I'm working on that, Marc. And I've got my people working on it. If it can't be done, then we'll live with that. But if we *can* move things forward a bit, Sanders says every week is critical at this point. And he of all people would know."

Shit. Just the news he didn't want to hear at this stage in the game. And he had no idea how to break that news to Dave.

Carla gave him a few moments to absorb the change in plans, and then continued on. There was so much that needed to get done, and so little time to do it. "You can assume that most of the pieces are going to be in place on my end. But one giant piece we need to resolve is the assignment of players to opposition assets, to the Dark Side. None of this will work unless we can get that finished, and we can't finish it, for obvious reasons, unless Dave is on board. Have you made any progress on that?"

Marc shook his head. "No. We've discussed it, and I've gone over the focus group charts with him. But that was just a few days ago. You can't expect him to get to the answer right away. He needs at least a little more time to absorb it and figure out the obvious solution."

"I've already told you, we don't have time." Carla's face had a dark and dangerous quality to it, a look he'd never seen on her before. "I need you to make this happen this week. By Friday, and not a day later. Our schedule is very tight, and everything hinges right now on that one problem."

"I'll get it done," promised Marc, resignedly. "I'll get Elle to help. He seems to trust her insight."

44

Elle had class on Tuesday morning, so Dave agreed to meet with her and Marc at the Einstein's Bagels shop on the Drag to go over what Marc said were some breakthrough ideas she had come up with regarding the Dark Side problem. Since it was early, he managed to find a parking space in the tiny lot just behind the store. Marc and Elle were already drinking coffee and nibbling on bagels when he walked in.

"Hey, Dave!" Marc called out. "I already ordered you a lox and bagels, and I got you a coffee right here."

"Sounds perfect, Marc. Morning, Elle." Dave dropped down in the booth opposite the two of them, picking up the cup of coffee Marc offered and taking a tentative sip. "So, Elle, thanks for taking time out for us this morning. Marc says you have some great ideas for solving the Dark Side problem."

"Sure." Elle shot him a melting smile. "First of all, I don't know if it will work, because I don't really know how the programming stuff works, but otherwise it seems like it might actually be doable."

"Okay, I'm all ears," Dave mumbled between bites of lox, cream cheese and bagel.

"Well, to start with, let's assume that the problem with the Dark Side is not game play. Opposition forces are not inherently less interesting because they're less fun to play."

"Generally speaking, I think that's a safe bet," Dave agreed. "Although in some cases we would have to goose up the model, make the weapons more powerful than they really are, because NATO forces are simply better equipped and trained than the other side. For instance, nothing in the Russian or Chinese air forces can possibly stand up to an F16 flown with full AWACS coverage."

"Right," Elle responded, somewhat cautiously. She had to tread carefully here. "And, more importantly, that difference would be largely invisible to players, anyway, particularly the first time they got assigned to the Dark Side. So, to be brief, that isn't our real problem here." She paused to take a sip of coffee, then continued. "It should be clear that the real problem is simply that the players don't feel comfortable even *pretending* to be on the Dark Side. That's especially true of being assigned to ISIS or Al-Qaeda. It's like being a child molester — even in a simulation, it just fees too *dirty* to enjoy it."

"Okay," Dave agreed, "so what do we do about it?"

"Again, this is just a suggestion, and I'm not sure you can even do it..." Elle noticed a brief look of annoyance cross Dave's face when she suggested he might not be able to *do* something, a response she was fully counting on. "But what if we simply have *everyone* play as NATO?"

Dave was confused. "Well, then we would have to make the computer simulate the opposition forces, and you've defeated the entire point of the game, that players are matched up against other live players."

"No, Dave," Elle explained, "what I'm saying is, say the game shows that every player is playing on the NATO side, against a Dark Side force. But that's all just an artifact. What if what they *see* in front of them is a Russian jet or Chinese ship or whatever, but what their opponent thinks he's controlling is *another* NATO jet or US Navy ship. They both *see* a Dark Side asset in front of them, and the back end server makes the translation."

Dave was slow to make the connection, but when it happened it was like a curtain falling open before him. "Of course! I mean, it isn't ideal from a game design perspective, but it could work." He started thinking through the various pieces of the puzzle. "So we could still have players opt in for the Dark Side, but if they choose not to, they can still be assigned to fight against a real NATO force, just without their knowing it. I'd have to build a translation module to map NATO weapons against their opposite Dark Side weapon, and figure out how that would play out during the game, but I think that's a brilliant solution!" He jumped up to give Elle a big hug, almost knocking over her coffee.

"I'm so glad we have you helping us, Elle," Dave gushed. "And helping Jules, too, this weekend. I don't know what we'd do without you."

Elle seemed pleased, as did Marc, who was beaming at her. "Just glad I can help, Dave. You know, I'm counting on the two of you to make us all rich."

"Well, this is certainly a giant step in that direction, Elle," Dave replied, pushing up from the table and grabbing his coffee and the remains of his bagel. "I've got to get back to the office and start working on this right now. It's just *brilliant*."

Dave was still muttering to himself, lost in thought as he walked out the back door of the restaurant to his car.

45

Carla was visibly relieved that the meeting at Einstein's had gone so well. "Yeah, Dave called and told me first thing this morning. Good work getting him on board with that." Marc had dropped Elle off at the business school, then hunted Carla down as soon as he got to the office to give her the news.

"It was really Elle who did all the heavy lifting. As soon as I explained the concept she got very excited about it, so I didn't have to do much to sell it to her myself." Marc dropped into the seat opposite Carla's desk. "I've been thinking about what you said about moving the launch date up. I don't have a problem with that, but we'll need to figure out how to handle creating demand for the game, and get it out to retailers on such short notice. None of that is trivial, but I talked to Elle about that after breakfast this morning and she offered to help me sort through all the tangles."

Carla walked over to where a copy of the launch calendar was hanging on the wall. "Okay, why don't we start with an arbitrary date and then work backward from there, to see where the snags are lying in wait for us." She pointed to the end of May. "Memorial Day would seem to be the absolute earliest we could launch. That means we would have to move the advertising up by a month at least, but since we are already so late into March, we're going to have to make some calls right away to see if that's even a possibility."

"Sounds about right," Marc agreed.

"Next," Carla continued, "we have to manufacture the disks and packaging, and move that through the supply chain to the stores in time for launch. That would be really tight — it forces us to complete the code like last week to get it cut, tested and packaged for shipment."

"And we still need to make the changes Dave agreed to this morning to get rid of the Dark Side problem," Marc suggested.

"That isn't a timeline issue, though. Those changes are going to be made on the back end, not the client code. And I think my people are already about ninety percent there, anyway."

"You moved ahead on that without even knowing whether Dave would go along with it?"

"Yeah, I had full confidence that you and Elle could close the deal on that one in time. And Sanders... you know." Carla pointed to the first of April. "So, anyway, our drop dead date on the client side is here, about a week away, which can't possibly be done." She looked pensive for a moment. "Unless—"

"Unless what?"

"Well, we already have some triggers built in to the client side to update code and pull down changes from the database. If we modularize the code a tad bit more, and strip out anything we don't actually need from the geo database, we could get the package size down to a single disk, and update that automatically when the user first logs into the game. In fact," she started scribbling notes on the whiteboard hanging next to the calendar, "we could strip out almost all of the geo, and just stream it as needed during the game. Our players have to be on a fat Internet pipe anyway, just to play, and the game isn't designed for offline action. I'll have to check on the math a bit, but I think it might actually work."

"I see what you're saying. We've been blinded to the fact that this is no longer a flight sim, where all the geo detail needs to be available at a moment's notice, so a player can enter a new location on the planet and immediately be transported to that place in full 4k detail. Now, we're the ones assigning them to a location, so we can just dump that location's data on them as needed. In fact, most of the action is on the sea or on the Russian steppes, or out in the middle of Syria, so we can give them fairly generic scenery and they'll never know the difference."

"Exactly. And this resolves some other issues we've been struggling with, as well. Like how to actually handle the back end translation of Dark Side weaponry into NATO equipment on the fly."

"Hmmm. It's worth considering. Let me get with Elle and check on how we'll handle the marketing angle, and you work out the coding issues with your team. Why don't we plan on regrouping in a few days to see if we can pull it off?" Marc got up to leave, then had a second thought. "Oh, and for the time being, we leave Dave out of this. He's already working full bore on getting the client code perfected, and I don't need him distracted. If we can work up a plan to speed up the launch, then we'll set up a meeting to sell it to him. Until then, we need to keep this just between us."

"Agreed. What's one more secret among friends?"

46

Two days later, Marc and Carla met for a working breakfast at Amaya's to discuss the possibility of an earlier launch date.

Marc got right to the point. "So, did you figure out whether we can have the code changes completed in time for a Memorial Day target launch?"

Carla pushed some sheets across the table at him. "The schedule's pretty tight, but if Sanders can find a little more money in the budget and free up some of his DOD assets, I think we can make it happen. Dave is almost done with his side, and our testers say the mapping is almost one hundred percent at this point. That guy is truly amazing."

"Yeah, well, when you put everyone else at Google to shame, it's a fair bet that you are without a doubt the best in the business." Marc glanced over the charts and timelines Carla had given him, whistling softly. "Speaking of amazing, you sure your guys can deliver on this?"

"If they don't, Sanders will have my ass. We'll *have* to make it work. The bigger question is, can you guys implement a marketing strategy that gets enough butts in the seats to make the project roll out as planned?"

"Elle and I have kicked this back and forth the last couple of days, and I think we've come up with a plan from way out in left field that might just do the trick." He quickly laid out the strategy for her.

Carla didn't know how to respond at first, so she took a few quiet moments to sip her coffee and sneak a bite or so off her breakfast taco. "It sounds crazy. I'll trust that you know what you're doing, but it just seems like it's all a bunch of smoke and mirrors."

"This whole project is smoke and mirrors, Carla. That's the magic of it."

Carla considered that. "So how are you going to get Dave on board? Does it even matter at this point? I mean, the client code is finished—"

"I don't want to hear that kind of talk, Carla." Marc was suddenly very serious, leaning toward her with a flare in his eyes. "Dave *has* to stay in the middle of this thing all the way through. You know what's at stake. What if there's a last minute glitch? Who the hell can fix it, who the hell knows the code better than Dave? Even *your* code? That issue is not on the table." Marc rested his hands flat on the tabletop. "This is Dave's baby. He was there for the birth, he's been there through all the growing pains, and he's going to be there at the finish. End of discussion."

"Okay, your call. So how do we sell it to him? You know how he reacted the last time we tried to move the launch date up."

"Right. But last time, Sanders kind of surprised me, and I didn't really handle it correctly. I jumped the gun with Dave, and had to find a way to walk it back. This time, we have the *gift* of time. As they say, timing is everything. So let's just move forward with our own timetables for a Memorial Day launch, and assuming we don't hit any speed bumps along the way, at the crucial moment I'll bring in a special — *consultant* — to sell the idea to Dave."

"The old 'consultant' ploy, eh?" Carla was finally buying into the strategy.

"Yep. Bring in an 'unbiased' outsider to deliver an 'expert' opinion on a controversial issue. Dave is from the programming side. He'll never see it coming."

"And who do you propose to deliver this unbiased expert opinion?" Carla arched her eyes, already guessing the answer.

"Why, of course, who could Dave trust more than... Elle."

47

Development continued at a feverish pace throughout the next few weeks. By the middle of April, Carla's team had almost completed work on the back end servers and were already diving into the online signup code. Elle was conducting focus group sessions twice a week to test the game and try out a variety of new marketing ideas. By the third week in April she asked Marc to set up a top-level meeting to review what she had learned and settle on the final plans for launch.

"Top o' th' morning to ya, Dave!" Marc motioned toward a plate of donuts and bagels and a large pot of coffee sitting on a side table. "Thought we might need some sugar and caffeine to get through it all." Elle was finishing up connecting her laptop to the flat screen monitor, and Carla was already chewing on a chocolate glazed.

"Sorry I'm running a little late," Dave apologized. "Traffic coming north from SoCo was a real bitch this morning."

"No problem." Elle smiled sweetly at him. "As you can see, I'm just getting things ready, myself. And Carla," she hooked a thumb at the dark-haired Goth, "is totally absorbed with making love to that donut."

"If only sex was half as good as this donut, I might be tempted to try it once in a while. Maybe even with a man." Carla's lips were completely coated with chocolate, but she didn't seem to care one bit.

"So is this everyone?" Dave asked, quickly surveying the room as he grabbed a chair.

"Yeah, just the chiefs. No Indians," Marc replied. "Elle has come up with some radical ideas, based upon what she's picked up from her focus groups. I, personally, think she's bat shit crazy. Maybe even affected by," Marc whispered conspiratorially, "*that time of the month*. But since I have to sleep with her, I had to call this meeting to let her rant. You know what that's like, Dave." Marc dodged quickly to the side to avoid Elle's punch, but still caught a slight glancing blow to his upper arm.

Elle shifted from a dark pretend scowl tossed in Marc's general direction to a more playful look. "Male chauvinist pigs aside, I think Carla and I would like to welcome you, Dave, to the more sophisticated adult dialog we have prepared for this morning." Carla beamed her approval, and Dave feigned a disapproving shake of his head in the direction of his friend. "Very well, then," Elle said haughtily. "Shall we continue with a more gender neutral discourse of our marketing research?"

"Go for it, sister!" Carla bellowed in response.

"Whatever," Marc responded in full but mischievous retreat.

Dave pressed his palms together and bowed deeply toward Elle in supplication. "I would personally like to apologize, Miss Elle, for my partner's barbaric and unrefined behavior. In his defense, he has been partaking recently of the local region's well recognized cultural obscenities of charred meat and country music, which have clearly left him emotionally retarded. I would think an immediate intervention, leading to a carefully supervised program of mani- and pedi-cures, might be necessary to restore this poor soul to his senses."

"Thank you, Doctor Elliott. Your treatment plan is well noted. I only hope we can still save him at this point." Elle glared at Marc theatrically, and he responded by clutching his heart and falling beseechingly to his knees.

"My apologies, my queen. But spare this knave my life and I will ever be your servant." Marc's over-the-top and well-scripted performance had accomplished its goal. Dave now seemed to be in a far more happy and receptive mood. And receptive was the key to this meeting.

"Very well, then," Elle continued. "I shall direct us to a less serious matter, that of our marketing focus groups." She clicked on the first PowerPoint slide. "As you know, the product testing has gone very well. We've had a few small bugs pop up, but nothing critical. And all of those were related to features that were still being fleshed out by the development teams." She glanced over at Carla and Dave, who were fully engaged, unusual for them when the topic veered any distance at all from their typical engineering issues.

"So the big items I wanted to cover this morning involve marketing and distribution issues." She clicked the pointer to move to the next slide. "As for marketing, our two biggest concerns are: A) building awareness, and B) building awareness. In other words, nobody out there knows that this game exists, and we have next to zero dollars available to change that, to build buzz for the game before launch."

Dave spoke up. "I thought we were going to start running ads for the game in a couple of the major gaming magazines."

"We are," Elle agreed. "But at the most we'll get in two months of ads before launch, and the advertising books say it should take six hits at a minimum before awareness sinks in. The problem is, there are just too many alternatives out there, too many other games to choose from. Too much advertising noise. And all of the ongoing games series, like *GTA* and *Fallout*, they get the lion's share of attention just because game buyers are familiar with the earlier versions."

"So what do you suggest we do about it?" Marc asked.

Another slide. "I think we need to get creative, think outside the marketing box for a change. We need to take our weaknesses, which I've listed here, and turn them into strengths."

Carla poured over the long list of challenges. "How do we take 'Untested product' and 'Unknown brand' and turn them into positives?"

"Well, the first step is to stop thinking like *us* and start thinking like *them*, like our target audience. *We* are all very busy, and we're all generally risk averse to trying new things. Plus we don't want to waste our time playing around with things that aren't quite ready." Elle swung her eyes around the table and saw that Marc and Carla were in agreement, as planned, but Dave wasn't quite sure where she was headed. "*They*, on the other hand, the gamers, they

227

spend their entire lives wasting time. That's what video gaming is all about, sinking all your free time into the unproductive pursuit of higher and higher scores. Something that puts zero food on the table at the end of the day." Dave signaled that he agreed with that point.

Elle continued. "In fact, our marketing research shows that gamers actually *like* being the guinea pigs for new, flawed products. They'll sign up to be alpha testers or beta testers of new products in a heartbeat. Think about all the people who dropped real money on the table to be one of the first testers for Google Glass." Dave knew all about that product, since he was a lead developer for the project. "So, here is the essence of my idea to build cheap buzz for our product launch: we give the game away to testers and call it a beta launch."

Elle paused to let the idea sink in around the table. Dave was the first to respond. "But if you give the game away, how will you ever make money? We're already pretty deep in the hole on this as it is."

"That's why I said we needed an *innovative* marketing strategy, one I like to call the—" Elle brought up the next slide, "Heroin Marketing Strategy. Like heroin, the first hit is free, but once you're hooked, you have to keep paying. Or in our case, playing. Actually, this isn't all that innovative. Razor blades work on this principle, as do ink jet printers, where just replacing the ink cartridges can cost almost as much as the printer itself. In fact, both Microsoft and Sony sell their game consoles at or below cost, and make their money off of licensing fees for games and online services."

"So down the road we sell them upgrades—" Dave was catching on.

"Improved weapons, add-ons, at some point even access to online play. The model for that has been in place for a long time now, with people actually paying real money to buy guns and swords in MMO games." Elle continued the slide show. "And we make a big deal out of this being a beta version. That way, even if we run into some problems at first, glitches in the game or slow-downs because the servers can't keep up, the players just mark it up to being on the edge, having exclusive access to a hot new game. "

Dave wasn't convinced. "Are you sure that will work, Elle? I mean, about launching it as a beta? You know what they say about pioneers. They're the ones with the arrows in their backs. And that has been especially true in the computer business. Microsoft has made a fortune out of fine-tuning other people's innovations."

Marc chipped in. "But here we won't be the pioneers, Dave. Remember that dinosaur game, Ark something or other? A guy quit Microsoft to create the first dinosaur-centered video game. A year later he launched it as an incomplete beta to beat the Jurassic World game to market, and they managed to beat Jurassic by about a week. Then, once the final version came out, they sold over two million copies right out of the chute. The beta primed the pump for the final version."

"Okay, Elle," Dave agreed, reluctantly. "I assume you've worked the numbers with Marc and they all pan out." Marc nodded and tapped a stack of papers in front of him. "But, still, how do we get the word out? And what about distribution? Do we still package it like a real game? What's in it for the retail stores?"

"Very good questions, Dave. Marc, do you want to handle the first one, getting the word out?"

"Sure." Marc stood up and took Elle's place at the head of the table. "As you guys know, I've been working with the guys at Microsoft on our advertising and packaging ideas, and it turns out they're getting ready for a blockbuster Xbox promotion this summer, cutting the price and bundling some extra games to clear out inventories of the current generation of consoles before they announce the Xbox Ultimate. It seems they got caught in the shorts the last time and had to eat a lot of Xbox 360s that nobody wanted to buy. It also helps them fend off any complaints from people bitching about how they paid full price for an Xbox One and now want a free upgrade to Xbox Ultimate."

"So how does that affect us?" Carla asked.

"Well, the MS guys put out an informal feeler to us about being part of the promotion. We would bundle our game for free with all new Xboxes sold, and they in turn would include promos of our game as part of their advertising and messaging. The stores would inventory our game for free, with truly outstanding placement and visibility in the store, since the game is such a big part of moving all the consoles."

230

"Just when is Microsoft planning to launch this new promotion?" Dave asked.

Bingo! Marc exchanged a quick look with Elle, who was sitting back appearing to be interested, even though they had spent the last three days rehearsing the sell. "That's the hitch, Dave. They're targeting the Memorial Day holiday weekend."

Dave exploded out of his chair. "But that's just a month away! How in the hell are we going to be ready for launch in just a month?"

Marc acted like he was stunned by Dave's outburst, but in fact it was exactly the response that he and Elle had counted on. "Hold on, Dave!"

"I *am* holding on! But you can't expect to drop a bombshell like that on me and have me just jump up and say 'oh goody goody'! Just how long have you known about this?"

"About a week," Marc lied. "And I didn't want to bother you with the idea until I checked into whether it would even work. But that's exactly why we're having this meeting. To get your ideas on whether we should tell Microsoft okay, or just tell them to go pound sand."

Elle cut into the heated back and forth. "Dave, this proposal from Microsoft would solve a lot of problems for us, both marketing-wise and financially. It would also ensure we get top-tier placement at the retail level. But none of that even matters if you and Carla can't meet the deadlines. This isn't about forcing a decision down your throat, it's about giving you some new options and getting your buyoff on whether those options are even feasible."

As usual, Elle's calm demeanor had a soothing effect on Dave. He excused himself to grab a Diet Coke down the hall, mainly just an effort to cool down and think things through. By the time he returned he already had a long list of new questions for them.

"Carla, what do you think? The code is still pretty far from being finished. How do we get that on disks and shipped out so close to going live? What about the sheer *size* of the database at this point? Do we even have the back end in shape enough to test whether the MMO handoffs will work?"

Carla paused to gather her thoughts. "Dave, this is all as new to me as it is to you." Marc was impressed with just how easily Carla could pull off that lie. "I'll need a day or so to think it through, but, just off the cuff, my gut says it's doable. We already have the hooks imbedded in the client side to handle code updates and changes to the database, so we could ship an alpha version of the game and update it at launch with the finished version. In fact, that would leave our development timeline pretty much the same as it was when we were targeting a July first launch."

Dave hadn't considered that idea before, but it made some sense. "Okay, but we'll still need to do something about the database size, Carla. It won't even fit on two Blu-Rays now."

"I've already been thinking about that, Dave. I think the real problem is, we've gotten caught up in a kind of database inertia. Think about it, we started this project by focusing on the flight sim database code, and never even considered what we would need on the database side to support an MMO game."

Dave's eyes suddenly lit up as he realized the technical implications of what Carla was saying. "So we can dump most of the database, and just download the geo data as we need it."

"Right! That will shrink the database size at least a hundred fold."

"And if we maintain a base level of detail for different generic locations, we can bluff our way through if the download is taking too long—"

"Exactly my thoughts, Dave. So what do you think? Shall we give the idea a day or so and see what we can do?"

Elle and Marc watched the interchange between the two code jocks silently, enjoying how skillfully Carla was luring Dave into her trap. And gentle Dave was the only one who had no inkling of what was happening.

Dave and Carla were buried deep in a technical discussion and seemed like they were about ready to bolt, so Elle held up her hand to stop them. "One last thing. We ran into an issue with one of our focus groups. Nothing about the program, Dave," Elle explained, responding to Dave's brief flash of concern. "It's about the name *Dronewars*. We've been using that name internally since day one, and I guess we've been assuming that would be the name we launched with. The problem is, and this came up in several of our marketing test sessions, the game is no longer just about drones. In fact, most of the weaponry has nothing at all to do with drones at this point. So the general consensus in our sessions was that the name is too confusing."

Dave was past caring about marketing issues at this point. "Elle, I don't really have any ownership on that. Anything you and Marc think will work is okay with me."

"Great! Glad that's not a problem." Elle let out a deep breath. "I would like everyone's vote on the final name, though. I've tested two options, and they both graded out about equal. So it's all up to us which one we go with."

Carla was checking her watch like she wanted to move along and get back to work on the accelerated launch date. "So, what are our choices, Elle?"

"The focus groups suggested either Virtual War or The Game of War."

Marc pitched in his opinion. "Virtual War seems too confusing to me. It might work with some geeks, but I don't see the appeal for the general audience. The Game of War, though, I like it. Reminds me of Game of Thrones. It never hurts to piggyback on an existing cultural reference, especially one with such a strong demographic overlap."

Elle turned toward Carla and Dave. "What do you guys think?"

Dave shrugged. "I'll go with whatever Marc likes. So unless you and Carla have some push back on it, The Game of War it is."

Carla indicated she had no opinion, and since Elle and Marc had already settled on the new name before the meeting, intentionally picking a bad second option to give Dave the illusion that he had a choice, the decision was made. The game would be launched as *The Game of War*. Marc couldn't help but chuckle to himself about the irony.

48

Carla had already worked out all the details to support an early launch, so over the course of the next day she simply spoon fed ideas to Dave, careful not to make her manipulation too obvious. In the end he bought in to the plan completely, and Marc called Sanders to give him the good news.

"You sure you can't make it any sooner?" Sanders demanded.

Give a camel an inch, and pretty soon he owns the whole damn tent. "No, Bob, Memorial Day weekend is slicing it pretty thin as it is. Plus, there's no way we can pull this off at all unless Microsoft comes through. I'm counting on you to deliver on that promise."

"That's a done deal, son. With the amount of money DOD spends with that crowd every year, they'll do back flips to keep us happy. You just keep your own people in line, and let me know if anything comes up that we need to handle." Sanders clicked off the video feed abruptly.

49

Dave and Carla worked miracles in the weeks leading up to launch, even creating a training mode for the game that could be used prior to the official launch to give players an opportunity to get used to the various elements of the game, in particular the customized user interface. Launch was set for 8 p.m. CDT on Memorial Day, which offered two major advantages. First, the timing was a little late for the east coast, but it insured that the maximum number of players would be available at launch time on the west coast. Second, since the game featured real-time weather and time zones, the game would start when it was daylight on the opposite side of the world. Where almost all of the game action would be played.

Dave woke up on launch day with a gnawing pain in the pit of his stomach. He had dedicated almost a year of his life to *The Game of War*, along with a substantial portion of his life savings, and it all came down to today.

There really wasn't much for him to do at this point. All of the code was complete, and the back end servers were in Carla's capable hands, Mark was busy keeping the help desk jumping, and Elle was handling last-minute press releases and responses to press inquiries. CNN and NBC had suggested a possible story later in the day, depending upon whether anything more interesting popped up, but Elle gave it only about a ten percent chance of actually happening.

Julia had to keep the shop open until late that evening to take advantage of the holiday shoppers that were already swamping SoCo, but she agreed to take a short break to join Dave for lunch. He picked her up out in front of the shop and, since the day had turned out sunny and very warm, they decided to head to a cluster of food trailers a few blocks over on South First Street. The food court was already packed, but after fighting to find a parking spot, Dave joined the back of the line for a Korean taco, and Julia went for her personal favorite, a barbecue vegetarian sandwich.

Even though Julia was eager to get back to the shop, she tried not to let it show. Dave looked like a child watching the clock on the last day of school, desperately needing some kind of distraction to make the time fly by faster. "Hey, why don't you go to a movie? It would be nice and cool in there, a good way to get out of the heat," Julia suggested.

"Thanks, Jules, but there isn't anything out right now I really want to see. Plus, it would be a sin to sit inside on the first pretty day we've had in a week." It had been raining non-stop for six days, but luckily for once the rain had not caused any major flooding.

"Then get out for a long walk, or take your bike down to Lady Bird Lake."

"Too muddy."

"You really are being quite impossible, you know," Julia pointed out, tossing a piece of lettuce at him.

Dave sat back on the bench, enjoying the moment and the playful smile Julia was beaming in his direction. "You know, Jules, there are moments like these that I really get what Pooh was trying to say."

"And what was that?"

"If you live to be a hundred, I want to live to be a hundred minus one day so I never have to live without you."

50

After dropping Julia off, Dave swung by the office to see if he could help out, but everything seemed to be moving along fine without him. He grabbed his tablet and went outside on the balcony to read, but the words seemed to swirl around in front of him, and finally he just gave up. He decided Julia was right about the movie, but he didn't want to be out of touch in case of an emergency, as unlikely as that now seemed, so he turned on Netflix and binge watched a few episodes of Doctor Who.

At a little after six, his cell phone chirped — a message from Elle. Her contact at CNN said their segment on the game launch would be airing in a few minutes. Dave switched over to CNN to watch, his stomach beginning to twist once again into knots.

A blonde female reporter was on the air, and at the bottom of the screen was the headline "Climate Change Upsets Mother Nature." He turned up the volume.

51

Wolff, climate change experts have been predicting for years that the rapid warming of the earth due to mankind's extensive release of greenhouse gases would eventually lead to significant disruptions in nature. We've already seen those effects in the form of violent and unprecedented storms over the last decade, and then the brutally cold weather that struck Europe this winter, but now it appears to be affecting even wildlife and sea life.

"I'm standing here on a pier a few miles north of Tokyo, Japan, where just this morning dockworkers reported seeing a huge pod of humpback whales breaching several hundred yards offshore. Similar sightings have been reported by fishermen and shore observers from as far north as South Korea to as far south as the South China Sea.

"What makes these observations interesting is the fact that these humpback whales are in the wrong location for this time of year. Humpback whales are migratory creatures, generally traveling over 16,000 miles in a single year. They feed only in summer, and only in polar waters, migrating to tropical or subtropical waters in the winter to breed and give birth.

"The scientists I talked to say these humpbacks should be much farther north by now, particularly the whales that have been seen in the tropical waters off Vietnam and Malaysia. They don't have an explanation for the phenomenon as yet, but several climate change experts have suggested that the ice melt off the polar ice caps may be desalinating the polar ocean water, and either disrupting the whales' built-in GPS homing system, or else affecting supplies of the krill and small fish that make up their primary diet.

"Adding to this mystery is the sudden appearance over the past few days of swarms of swan geese migrating across China. Swan geese are almost entirely domesticated, although some have been known to go feral from time to time. Historically, however, the wild population is very small, and no one seems to have any idea where these swan geese have been nesting over the winter months. More importantly, no one has ever seen such massive numbers of swan geese migrating northward for the winter. But the sudden increase in the Asian goose population appears to mirror what we've seen in North America, where Canadian and North American goose populations have increased over twenty fold since 1970. And those climate change experts I spoke with say this is only the beginning of a massive change in animal behavior — and animal populations — around the world."

The picture switched to Wolff Blitzer, nattily dressed in a dark grey suit and blue tie. "Mother Nature continues to surprise us all, Kelley." He turned slightly to his left to face the camera. "Meanwhile, in business news, a small start-up in Austin is offering its own surprises. Founded by two former programmers from Google, little Rocketship Games is poised to make video game history tonight with the launch of the largest multiuser game ever. Their game, called *The Game of War*, was released just last week for

242

users to play in an offline mode. Even with that limited functionality, it has been earning rave reviews from game bloggers and Internet web sites across the country. What makes this game even more impressive is that, in an industry where new game titles typically take armies of programmers working for several years and spending many millions of dollars, Rocketship produced this game in less than a year with just two programmers and $20,000 raised online in a Kickstarter campaign. Will it work? Well, no one is sure, but in just a little less than three hours we'll all find out whether this Rocketship is going to soar, or instead will simply flame out, crash and burn."

My money's on the first one, Dave silently prayed.

liftoff

52

The crabs crawling up on shore out of the Bay of Sevastopol were black with subtle streaks of green, brown and sand. They scuttled quickly across the ground, searching for protective cover. All around them, Russian seamen and other dock workers continued about their business, unmindful of the silent invasion.

53

Carla checked and re-checked the servers, even creating a fault condition in one of them to test the failover cluster, which worked flawlessly to automatically switch the workload on the failed server to another server in the cluster. The fat pipe Internet connection to the collocation facility at the University of Texas showed a throughput of 200 gigabits per second, overkill for what they needed, but the new medical school would surely find a use for that capacity down the road. She glanced at the clock. *Another two hours.*

54

The Chinese aircraft carrier *Liaoning* was steaming northeast in the South China Sea, just west of the Spratly Islands. China purchased the *Liaoning* from Ukraine in 1998, then spent four years refurbishing the flattop at Dalian, a shipyard in northeast China. Deployed all around her was a carrier battle group of three Type 052D destroyers, two of the newer Type 055 destroyers and four Type 054A frigates. Patrolling nearby were two Type 093 Shang nuclear submarines.

Only one support ship had joined the group, which highlighted one of China's most glaring naval weaknesses. The country had committed to a fast-paced program to modernize its navy, augmenting its refurbished Soviet-built ships like the *Liaoning* with newer designs largely stolen from the United States Navy. What they ignored in their naiveté was the critical importance of support ships — mostly tankers, dry stores vessels and ammunition ships. Without support ships, a carrier group running low on jet fuel, ammunition or food would have to return to port to resupply, severely limiting the group's ability to project force at a distance.

The *Liaoning* carrier group was currently tasked with enforcing the South China Sea no-fly zone that Beijing had announced just three days earlier. Assisting the carrier were naval and air force assets deployed on artificial islands China had recently constructed in the Spratley and Paracel Islands. To the north, another Chinese carrier group was patrolling the seas off Taiwan. China had used the arrival of a United States Navy littoral combat ship off the Vietnamese shoreline as an excuse to heighten tensions in the area, but many analysts in SEATO and NATO were concerned that the moves were simply a pretext for a planned invasion of Taiwan.

Down in the sonar room, pings began to blossom on the sonar screens, showing several large shapes rising up from the deeper ocean waters to the north. The sonar operators began to panic, until they finally picked up the distinctive sounds of whale calls coming from the direction of the sonar returns.

55

Now that the spring semester at the graduate business school was finally over, Elle had committed to helping Marc full time on the launch. With thirty minutes to go before they finally pulled the switch, everything seemed to be a go.

Carla reported in that the servers and Internet connections were all at peak condition, and thousands of players were still in the final stages of downloading the code. Dave was a wreck in his office, going out of his mind with nothing to do but wait. Marc had the support center already responding to minor problems with the sign-up process.

56

The sky was slowly brightening with streaks of pink and gold, even though the sun had not yet climbed above the black horizon. Normally the Kurdish sentry's binoculars were trained to the southeast, where the major threat from remnants of ISIS still lay. But periodically he would sweep the entire perimeter for other threats, and the dark smear that was developing on the northern horizon was starting to worry him. The weather forecasts had called for clear skies all week, but that was looking more and more like a major storm. He called in the observation to his radar unit, who reported that it appeared to be some kind of amorphous mass, with particles much too small to be aircraft but too large to be water droplets. They didn't seem at all concerned.

The northern sky blackened quickly as the mass swept toward them. The rest of the Kurdish soldiers had begun to point excitedly toward the sky, and many stopped to ready their weapons, just in case. An anti-aircraft battery trained its sights to the north, not believing the reports from the radar crew.

Just fifteen minutes after the first sighting, the mass swooped overhead, and the Kurdish soldiers got their first clear view of what appeared to be an enormous flock of large black birds, all headed south. The flock spread across the sky all the way from the eastern to the western horizons, and as far to the north as they could see.

57

The clock ticked to 8 pm CDT. All across the country, Xbox players started receiving data on their assigned weapons and missions. *The Game of War* had started.

the game of war

58

The Chinese sailors on the flight deck of the carrier watched as a pod of twelve humpback whales crested the surface, ocean water streaming down their blue-black sides. Suddenly, one of the whales spewed a geyser of water from its blowhole. One by one the other whales followed suit. The sailors had never seen anything so utterly majestic.

A sentry posted on the carrier's conning tower trained his binoculars on the whale closest to the carrier group, watching the water cascading down the side of the whale and back into the ocean. *What strange skin*, the sentry thought. *It almost doesn't look real.*

59

Dave had been monitoring the startup of the game on several flat screen displays mounted on the wall of the central control room. The game appeared to be scaling up nicely, the servers handling the rapidly increasing game volume with no apparent problems, and the latency numbers were showing no unsurprising delays in the game action. But Dave couldn't shake the feeling that something was... *wrong*.

It took him a few minutes to figure it out, and Dave could kick himself when he did. *The total players. No way that number is right.*

He reached into his pocket for his cell phone. "Carla? This is Dave in the control center. I've picked up something that doesn't smell right. When you add up the total numbers of players on all sides, the result is just too big. That's way more than the number of games we've sold. In fact..." He quickly rechecked the screens. "We're now showing almost twice as many players as we should."

"Let me look into it and I'll get right back to you," Carla answered.

His phone buzzed not five minutes later. "You're right, Dave, there seems to be some glitch that's causing the player numbers to be double- or triple-counted. If you think it's critical I can get someone on it tonight, but with all this volume I'd prefer staying focused on maintaining the server balance to keep the latency numbers in line, and wait to check on the counters until later on in the morning."

258

"Yeah, that's fine," Dave murmured. "I just don't know how that happened, and why we didn't see it earlier. But tomorrow's fine. No worries."

"Thanks, Dave. And, by the way, wow, congratulations! It is really happening!"

"Well, congratulations are still a little premature, Carla, but thanks. We still need to get through this first night before we crack open the bubbly." Still, the numbers up on the boards, even dividing by two or three, grossly exceeded his wildest dreams. Dave had a momentary flashback of Sally Fields shouting "You like me!" at the Academy Awards. After all those years slaving away in virtual obscurity at Google, Dave was finally getting his day in the sun.

60

Todd was deeply engaged with the screen in front of him, his Boeing AH-64 Apache helicopter seemingly hovering in place just to the left of his primary target. The threat assessment matrix, located at the top right hand corner of the screen, showed the primary target and several alternate targets, all now outlined in yellow.

He checked the weapons stores matrix, laid out in the top left hand corner. The WSM showed he was carrying a load of four 70mm folding-fin aerial rockets and 100 30mm rounds for his M230 automatic cannon. *That seems a little light,* he thought, double checking the expected weapons capacity for the Apache on his cell phone while he waited for the targets to glow red. *Strange. The Apache is supposed to carry way more rockets and ammo than that. Guess it's just part of the game.*

61

S hit. How did we miss that?" Sanders swore to himself as he stomped down the hall, clutching his phone tightly in his left hand. Still, in the end it changed nothing. He ordered Carla to dummy up a bug in the code to explain the problem, assuming this went on long enough for it to matter. He just didn't need to deal with Dave poking his head in the code right now and raising more questions. Not tonight.

More importantly, the intel he was getting back from the field indicated everything was going according to plan. No, that wasn't right — everything was blowing the plan numbers completely out of the water. He already had more players online than he had assets for them to manage, and Carla's team had to switch some of the incoming players over to the real game servers. It wasn't a scenario they had really planned for, but she was doing a great job handling it nonetheless.

Sanders checked his watch as he stalked past a Marine guard and into the control room. The President would be expecting an update very soon.

62

Brandon brought his submarine up to the water's surface, his assigned target dead in front of him. The ship was steaming almost directly toward him from the southwest. He glanced at the distance indicator. *Almost there. Just a few more seconds...*

63

Despite Carla's reassurances that nothing was wrong on the server side, that it was all just a counter glitch, Dave still couldn't shake the nagging feeling that something wasn't right. He couldn't afford for any server problems to pop up at the last minute that would shut down the game, or even cause persistent lags in the action. They had one chance to get this launch right, and any mistakes would likely kill the game at birth.

Then he remembered the test version of the back end server monitoring code he had built into the client program months earlier, before the real back end servers were operational. In theory, every copy of the program currently running should be pinging his development box with basic status updates every minute or so. He found the icon for the monitoring program on his computer desktop and double-clicked it.

64

The crabs scurried across the ground at a surprisingly high speed, each of them eventually finding shelter beneath tanks, armored personnel carriers, and other ground-based weapons. A sailor kicked at one crab that had gotten too close, but missed.

Back in Sevastopol Bay, large dolphins suddenly appeared, rising up from the depths and swarming around the Russian naval ships docked at the Sevastopol port.

65

The numbers weren't even close! According to Dave's old monitoring software, there were four times as many players online as Carla's software was showing. And instead of the players being evenly split between NATO and Dark Side, almost all of the players were on the NATO side. Dave double-checked his code to be sure, but everything checked out. Something was *very* wrong!

66

The targeting indicator on Todd's screen suddenly glowed bright red. A small dark hole appeared in the simulated ground in front of him, followed almost immediately by a tall burst of flame gushing skyward. Todd watched as moments later the nose of a Russian RS-24 Yars ballistic missile rose slowly out of the hole, its speed growing with every second. He fixed his gun sight on the body of the missile and launched two of his 70mm folding-fin aerial rockets.

One rocket missed, but the other tore into the carbon fiber skin of the missile and detonated. A second later the entire missile exploded, rocking his Apache helicopter backward with its blast wave.

Todd swung the Apache right to engage the next target. The missile was already out of the silo and climbing, but he flipped his weapons selector to the Hughes M230 Chain Gun, firing several bursts of its 30mm rounds into the missile at point-blank range. The target exploded immediately, causing shards of the missile and flames from the explosion to rip through his helicopter, destroying it in seconds.

His screen went blank momentarily, but a few seconds later it lit back up with the simulated cockpit of another Apache helicopter. This time the target ahead was a MZKT-79221 mobile missile launcher for a Russian Topol-M ballistic nuclear missile. As he watched, the missile was quickly being ratcheted into launch position. He made a split-second decision to fire his rockets into the erector mechanism of the launcher, destroying the erector and causing the missile to crash back down onto the bed of the launcher. The Topol-M employed a solid-fuel three-stage booster, capable of reaching targets up to 6,500 miles away. As it landed on the launcher off-kilter, the bottom half of the booster split apart. Todd backed his Apache away, then fired tracer rounds into a rapidly yawing opening in the booster's skin. The propellant ignited violently, and within moments the missile was completely destroyed.

Todd checked the threat assessment matrix again. Another two targets were glowing red off to his right.

67

Dave picked up his cell to call Marc, but his partner wasn't answering, so he left a short voice message, then added a brief text message telling Marc that he was heading to the server room to check on how things were going. He shot a similar message to Carla.

The servers were located in a secured room on the second floor. A single door accessed the server room, and there were no windows to the outside, reducing the risk of weather-related incidents and helping to maintain stable temperatures throughout the room. Dave swiped his badge against the electronic lock, and the door lock clicked, letting him inside.

68

Kevin kept his MQ-9 Reaper low over the water to stay below the Russian radar coverage. The Reaper had launched as a group of four drones from the eastern tip of Turkish Cyprus and was rapidly closing in on its target, the Hmeymim air base in Latakia, Syria, on the Mediterranean Sea. Hmeymim was the strategic headquarters for Russia's military operations in Syria.

His display showed six minutes to target. He flipped his weapons selector to Hellfire missiles.

69

The server arrays were made up of twenty Dell PowerEdge M820 blade servers, mounted in a standard Dell NetShelter SX 42U Rack Enclosure. The servers were redundant and hot-swappable, so a single server failure, while rare, would have little overall impact on players — in the event of a server failure the load would simply be picked up by its mirrored server and an alarm would go off to notify the server support crew. Extra blades — standalone computers in special enclosures that made them easy to install or remove from the server racks — were stored off to the side, along with replacement solid state disk drives and memory modules.

The servers were routed through a Cisco 12006 router to the main University of Texas collocation facility, which was housed in a nondescript building on the east side of the main campus. The UT colo was itself connected to one of the main trunk lines for the Internet, so Internet throughput would not be a bottleneck for Rocketship's server array. *The Game of War* was running on the fattest pipe possible.

A single monitor served all twenty computers, connected to a Dell Digital KVM 32-port monitor switch. Quickly scanning the status lights on the blade array to make sure nothing was obviously amiss, Dave keyed in his user ID and password, then tapped the keyboard to bring up an administration console for Blade #1.

70

The Chinese sailors were gathered on the railings around the deck of their destroyer, watching the whales with avid fascination. Once again the whales began to spew geysers of water in the air. This time, however, just as the fountains of water reached their peaks, the whales began to roar.

Suddenly, out of the top of each of the geysers shot clusters of missiles, trailing smoky exhaust flames as they arched over toward the Chinese ships, now lolling helplessly like sitting ducks in the water.

In seconds the carrier group was devastated by the missile attack. Sailors raced to try to contain the damage, but the destruction was too widespread. The carrier *Liaoning* had been struck in multiple locations on its starboard side just below the water line, and was rapidly taking on water. In minutes it began to list as the sailors abandoned their repair efforts and sprinted for the lifeboats.

71

Yes! Brandon watched gleefully while the missiles he had launched from his submarine picked apart the Chinese ships with deadly accuracy. Firing from such close range, the Chinese had no opportunity to activate their anti-missile defenses before they were completely decimated. Other submarines in his group had launched missiles, too, and soon the entire Chinese carrier group was headed for the bottom of the ocean.

After a short delay, Brandon's screen flickered, and he was rewarded with a new target lying dead ahead. It appeared to be some kind of shipyard. He couldn't tell if the letters on the ships and surrounding buildings were Chinese or Japanese, but his threat assessment matrix showed several targets ahead, all glowing bright red. He checked his weapons. *A full load of missiles. Like shooting fish in a barrel.*

72

arc's phone was on silent and his smartwatch was out of power, so as a result he had missed Dave's urgent call. But Carla, sitting directly across from him, immediately picked up on Dave's text message, letting her know that he was on his way to the server room. "Marc, we've got a big problem!" she sputtered, alarm lighting up her eyes. "It's Dave!"

Marc glanced down at his phone, instantly seeing that he had missed both Dave's call and his text message. He opened the message, and his eyes widened like saucers. Jumping up, he shouted "Follow me!" to Carla, and hit speed dial for Sanders.

Sanders answered on the second ring. "Bob, we've got a situation," Marc spit out, already racing for the stairs. The elevator would be too slow. "Dave's somehow caught on to something, and he's headed for the server room. If he gets in there, and gets onto the servers, he's gonna know right away that something is wrong."

"How the hell does he still have access to the server room?" Sanders was livid. "That should have been shut down before this even started!"

"I know," Marc explained, already a little out of breath as he and Carla darted up the stairs. "But locking him out would have raised a big red flag, too. This *is* his program, after all. If he had tried to get in there and it was sealed, he'd have raised a huge fuss. As it is, maybe we can keep this locked down."

"If you know what's good for you, you *better* lock it down! Whatever it takes!"

"Yessir, I'm on it." Marc burst through the door at the top of the stairs. The server room was just down the hall and to the left. He keyed the red End button on the phone to hang up the call, and grabbed Carla as she reached the second floor right behind him.

"Get in there and stop him!" Marc ordered. "I'll listen from out here in case there's a problem. We need to get Dave out of there before he finds out what's really happening!"

Carla nodded gravely, grabbing her key card to unlock the door to the server room.

73

The black cloud split into two parts, with half of the birds veering to the east, toward Iraq, and the other half continuing south and west into Syria. Every now and then, a few birds would break away from the flock and swoop down, taking deadly aim at an unsuspecting victim. As they leveled out near the ground, the birds opened up with 7.62mm Vulcan miniguns, banking sharply to the left and right and shredding the ISIS soldiers at point blank range.

Even firing short bursts, at a rate of over 2,000 rounds per minute the miniguns were quickly silenced, and the birds were left with no option but to valiantly sacrifice themselves by smashing into the nearest armored target. Mounted on the nose of each bird was a 5.9 kg shaped explosive, designed specifically to penetrate the skin of tanks and armored personnel carriers. The two flocks swept inexorably across the sands of the Levant, leaving a bloody, smoking swath of devastation in their wake.

74

*S*trange, Dave thought, *this should be running at close to full tilt, with all the users we have connected to the game, but it seems to be almost idle.* He keyed CTRL-ALT-DEL, and clicked on Task Manager. The list of running applications checked out fine, but when he clicked on Performance, it looked like the computer was barely doing anything. The CPU was running at about 10%, Memory was at 6% and Disk Access was almost zero. More importantly, the Ethernet connection should have been blowing up with all the simultaneous connections to — he quickly calculated — around ten thousand users for this one box, but the Ethernet traffic was at baseline. *This can't be right.* He flipped to the second blade, then the third. Every server was showing the exact same thing — they were all sitting idle.

Dave flipped over to the Cisco router console, again keying in his user ID and password to get through security to its admin screen. *Almost zero traffic! What the f-*

Suddenly the door burst open behind him, and Dave spun to see Carla standing in the doorway. She shut the door behind her, staring at him with a quizzical expression. "Dave, I was just coming up to check—"

"Carla, what the hell is going on here?" Dave exploded. "The game, the back end servers, none of that is being run through here. It's like this is all nothing but a goddamned mock-up!"

75

Kevin pulled the nose of his Reaper up, gaining altitude at the last possible moment to skim just above the tree tops. The drone's AN/AAS-52 Multi-Spectral Targeting System showed his target dead ahead, a Russian S-400 Triumf anti-aircraft battery. His gunsight started flashing red. *Time to unload*, he thought, releasing his four Hellfire missiles one after another. He watched as the Hellfires streaked toward the target at close to a thousand miles per hour. In moments the missiles struck pay dirt, obliterating the air base's anti-aircraft defenses.

Kevin pulled his nose up a little more and selected his two GBU-12 Paveway II laser-guided bombs. The base's runways were straight ahead. He aimed his targeting laser for the center of the first runway and fired, then switched to the second runway and fired again. *Now their jets are useless, too,* he noted with satisfaction.

The other three Reapers in his group were similarly busy. In just minutes they had eliminated the Russian air defense capability. Behind them, four F16 Fighting Falcons swooped in to complete the devastation.

76

In the blink of an eye, Carla scanned the graphs on the server monitor, all of which clearly indicated that no significant Internet traffic was coming in or out of the server room. *Shit! He knows.* "Dave, it's not what you think—"

Dave grabbed her roughly by the shoulders. "I repeat, *Carla*, what the hell is going on? This is all a sham... these servers, they might as well all be shut down. What the *hell* is going on with the game?"

Carla shrugged out of his grip and moved toward the monitor, desperately trying to come up with an answer to Dave's questions. And failing. "Dave, I don't know what you're talking about. The game is running at full speed. Maybe you misread—"

"I *know* how to check the workload on a computer, Carla. These servers are running at idle, and there is zero traffic on the router."

Carla shook her head, not knowing how to respond. Maybe she should just tell him the truth at this point—

"Where's Sanders?" Dave demanded. "I'm gonna find that son of a bitch and get some answers out of *him!*"

Dave had his back to the door when a voice behind him growled, "You're not going anywhere."

Dave turned around, and saw him standing in the doorway, a gun pointed casually and lethally at Dave's chest. Marc. "You're not going anywhere," he repeated.

77

What the hell *is* this? A *gun*? You've got a *gun*?" Dave was stunned, the room starting to spin a little in front of him.

"Don't worry, Dave, no one is going to shoot you. We just need you to cooperate for a little while longer," Marc explained, lowering the weapon slightly.

"Somebody please tell me what's *happening!*" Dave's entire world had been shattered in just moments. He staggered toward a chair sitting just to his right, collapsing into it.

Marc tried a calming tone of voice. "Dave, I can't tell you everything right now. Just trust me that everything's okay. We've got it all under control."

"*Trust* you?" Dave was exasperated. "*Trust* you? Right now I don't even know who you *are!*" Dave pointed toward the gun. "How can I *trust* someone who's ready to shoot me?"

Marc pulled a chair up in front of Dave and sat down. "I'm not going to shoot you Dave. I just need you to sit there and listen for a moment."

"No, I'm not going to sit here. I'm going to find out what's really going on around here!"

Marc hung his head, his hand still firmly in control of the gun in his lap. "I can't let you do that, Dave. Not yet. For now you just need to stay in here and not cause trouble."

"So now I'm a *prisoner*?"

"No, not a prisoner. I just need you to sit still and not cause a fuss. Too much is riding on this, Dave. Too many lives are at stake to screw this thing up."

While Marc was talking, Carla had eased closer to Dave. Suddenly, she whipped out her hand and grabbed Dave's cell phone out of his left pocket.

"What the—" Dave made a desperate grab for his phone, but Carla was too quick. "Give that back, you bitch!"

Marc his head slowly. "You'll get it back later, Dave. Right now I can't let you start calling people. This has to stay under wraps for a few more hours." Marc took the phone from Carla. "Carla, go let Sanders know I've got things under control."

Carla gave him a thumbs up and quickly slipped out the door.

"Dave, you asked for answers." Marc paused a moment to set the safety on the pistol. "I can't tell you everything at this point, not for a few more hours. But I can give you the big picture."

Dave was glaring at him, his anger still barely in check. "Okay, then. Start talking."

78

The Port of Sevastopol was in flames. The sudden and simultaneous detonation of the crab drones had left most of the Russian ground defenses in shambles, and even the weapons that had survived the initial attack, like the Russian T-14 Armata tanks, were next to useless in the chaos that followed.

The sailors aboard the Russian warships in the port were standing around, paralyzed with uncertainty, when the dolphin drones began to detonate in the water alongside their boats. Several ships were compromised immediately and began settling into the water, while other Russian crewmen fought furiously to stanch the flow of seawater streaming into their ships.

As the Russian commanders struggled to regain control of the situation and organize their repair teams, American Predator and Reaper drones appeared from out of the bay to the south. Simultaneously, Ukrainian army forces attacked from the north, and Ukrainian paratroopers began landing on the outskirts of Sevastopol.

79

Marc wiped his brow, pausing for a moment to catch his breath. "Where do I begin?"

"Why don't you start with whatever's happening right now. Why these servers aren't working. What's going on with the game," Dave demanded.

"Okay... I don't know all the details, Dave, but I do know the shape of things from thirty thousand feet—"

"Get on with it." Dave had long run out of patience.

"Yeah, well, starting with the servers. These servers were actually never intended to do anything. They were just a ruse to keep you from suspecting the truth about the game."

"What truth?"

"I'm getting to that, Dave." Marc pointed toward the server array. "You see, these servers in here are an order of magnitude too small to cover the horsepower we needed for the game. Maybe even more than that. The actual back end server array is *massive*."

"What do you mean, the *actual* server array? Where the hell is that?"

"Carla and her group figured out pretty early on that the scale of the game, when it launched, would demand a huge dedicated server room, and an Internet connection that dwarfed what is normally available in commercial or residential areas. Even gigafiber connections are way too slow — we needed about a hundred times that much bandwidth."

"But that's impossible," Dave pointed out. "The only way to get that much bandwidth is to lay down a custom direct connection to the Internet trunk lines. So the servers would either have to be located at the University of Texas collocation facility, or you'd have to lay a dedicated fat pipe from your server room straight to UT."

"Exactly, Dave. And that's just what they did."

"That's impossible," Dave reiterated. "There's no way you could do that without tearing up the streets and—" Suddenly he understood. "The medical school."

"That's right, Dave. Sanders has been preparing for this for years. When UT got approval to build a new medical school in Austin, he saw his one chance to invest in some improved infrastructure. That's the real reason they had to dig up Red River Street. To lay down new fiber."

"And the server room is located somewhere in the medical school complex." It all suddenly made perfect sense.

"Exactly. When UT started drawing up plans for the new medical complex, they intentionally grabbed all of the real estate they could get their hands on, making room for the future. They didn't need all those buildings for just fifty medical students, so that left lots of extra capacity. Sanders moved fast and grabbed some of it right from the start. And not just for the servers — the programming staff working on the back end servers alone numbered in the hundreds."

Dave had wondered how Carla's little group had made so much progress so fast. "So she had an army working away on the back end—"

"Yes, Dave. And she had years to get it done, to hone the back end down to a fine science."

Dave was still struggling to understand all of this. "But why? What was the purpose of it all? Why would Sanders and whoever he's working for care about a goddamned game?"

"Because it wasn't really *The Game of War* after all, Dave." Marc paused and leaned forward slightly. "It was a real war."

Dave tried to soak that in. *A real war? What the f-* "And so who the hell are you, then?" he demanded.

"I'm Marc Cullen, all right. But I was never really with Google. That part was faked."

"Okay, then, who exactly *are* you working for?"

Marc looked Dave straight in the eyes, unflinching. "I'm from a blacks ops section of the DIA. Military intelligence. Sanders is my section head. My boss."

80

The tension of the past few days was finally catching up with Sanders as he clicked off the conference call connection with the President and his team of military advisers, all huddled together in the Situation Room of the White House to monitor the progress of the war. The call had gone well. Very well. Beekeeper had succeeded beyond anyone's wildest expectations, with every single major objective accomplished and limited casualties to fret over.

Seven Russian sea-launched intercontinental ballistic missiles had slipped past their drone net. Three of those missiles were targeted for Los Angeles, Chicago and Miami, and the other four were aimed at America's own ballistic missile fields in New Mexico and South Dakota. The anti-ballistic missile defense teams had prioritized neutralizing the missiles aimed at the cities, and successfully knocked all them out of the air well short of their targets. Two of the other ICBMs got through and scattered MIRV nuclear warheads across wide but barren swathes of New Mexico and the Dakotas. There was some loss of life, and the radiation would have to be dealt with at some point, but all in all, not a bad tradeoff for wiping out Russia's entire nuclear arsenal. Or at least enough to make sure they were no longer a threat.

The Ukrainian army was also experiencing limited casualties as they moved rapidly east and south to recapture Crimea and Sevastopol. But their losses were nothing compared to how they would have fared against a Russian force fighting at full strength. Meanwhile, the South Korean army was marching unmolested toward Pyongyang.

And as for the Chinese, Sanders chuckled to himself, the next Chinese navy would need to buy a fleet of glass bottomed boats. *To search for the first Chinese navy*

81

As Marc laid out the long series of lies and deceptions he had pulled off over the past year, Dave was flabbergasted.

"So the CES demo was all a fake?" Dave demanded.

"No, that was real, just not in the sense you thought it was. There were several other pilot groups in the project. Three others, in fact. Each of us had identified a programmer we thought had the talent and experience to get the job done. Sanders gave us some time to put together a demo, using it as a showcase for what we could pull off, given the constraints of having to do it all with just the Prepar3D SDK. The timelines were tight, and the plan was for all of us to meet at CES in Vegas as cover for the competition, to see which team would continue forward. Obviously, we — you — won."

"And Dovetail?"

"Yeah." Marc let out a little laugh. "That was all show, although I didn't know it at the time. Sanders needed you fully on board with the Lockheed relationship, and he thought the best way to do that was to convince you there was no other way out of the hole you'd dug. And it worked, too. There were a lot of moments over the last few months where you might have caught on to what was really going on around you, if you had really been paying attention. But by jumping into bed so deep and so fast with Lockheed, by the time you might have questioned how much they had taken control of the project, it was too late for you to back out."

"Are you saying the meeting in New York was just a scam?"

"All Hollywood, Dave. We evidently never even talked to Dovetail at all. Sanders just needed to get that option out of the way for you, leaving Lockheed as the only possible partner."

"So, in the end, this entire project was all orchestrated by Lockheed," Dave suggested.

"No, actually, they were mostly just dupes as well. Sanders pulled some strings at the Pentagon to get the flight sim group at Lockheed temporarily assigned to him, under the pretext that we were developing some black ops software. Which, I guess, we were. Carla, of course, was from our team, and inserted into the Prepar3D team at about the same time Sanders took over."

"But *why*? Why go to all the trouble to pretend they were Lockheed?"

"Because, Dave, that was the only way to make the story believable, to keep you in the dark about what was really going on. Everyone knew that Microsoft had licensed the flight sim code to Dovetail and Lockheed. So Sanders knocked off Dovetail at the start, leaving only Lockheed. And Lockheed's military connection worked to convince you that the changes to *Dronewars*, adding in all the new weapons systems and retargeting the game toward the Russians and Chinese, were all legitimate. Incrementally, step by step, we gradually moved you from *Dronewars* to *The Game of War*. And you had no idea what was really going on behind the scenes."

"Why did we have to change the name at the last minute?" Dave wondered.

"Oh, that came from the intel guys at DIA. They thought calling it *Dronewars*, with all the publicity from the pre-launch marketing, might accidentally send a signal to the other side about what we were up to. I guess we should have thought about that earlier on, but I almost had to laugh when I told you we needed to change the name because the game was no longer about drones. In fact, the whole exercise was code-named Operation Beekeeper. Because, just like with real live beehives, all the work was done by the drones."

Dave let that soak in. People had been talking about wars fought by robot soldiers for decades. The *Terminator* movies were a perfect example of that. But those robots were almost always depicted as mechanical *men*. In reality, the first robots used in war evidently looked nothing at all like men. "So in the end, what is really happening tonight? What did I really help to build?"

"Well, Dave, the thing to remember is, it wasn't just a game. All the time you thought you were creating a massive drone warfare simulation, you were actually creating a massive control system for real drones. The so-called simulated targets were all real targets, real ships and nuclear missiles and armored personnel carriers. While we're sitting here, over one hundred thousand 'players' are busily guiding their drones — on land, in the air and in the oceans — toward actual enemy military assets. Targeting and destroying them. As of eight o'clock our time tonight, the United States initiated World War III against all of its major enemies. By midnight we will have won."

"And you need me safely locked up until the shooting stops."

"That's the gist of it. Nothing personal, Dave. But right now thc other side has no real inkling of what's actually happening, and we need to keep it that way. Plus we need to keep all those pimply-faced video gamers hard at work blasting the Russians and the Chinese back into the last century. The one thing we can't risk at this point is for anyone to find out what is really going on. Not until this thing is over."

"You guys are insane. There's no way this can work!"

"That's where you're wrong, Dave. It *is* working. And the fact that I've been sitting here talking to you for so long without a single call from Sanders means it's working very well."

"Who else was in on this? The Lockheed guys? *Julia*?"

"No. Just Carla and me. And Sanders. Carla to manage the connection to her back end code, and me to keep driving the project toward its logical conclusion, with a push every now and then from Sanders to point me in the right direction. Everyone else was just a passenger. Just like you. Actually, not like you, because *you* were the key piece to the puzzle, the magic that made the whole front end software work. That's why I was sent to recruit you from Google. And you succeeded beyond our wildest expectations."

"So where do we go from here?"

"For the next few hours, I'll post a guard to make sure you stay put. Carla's already shut down the Internet connection from in here, so there's no way for you to get a message out. And, before you start protesting, that's for *your* protection. If word of any of this somehow slips out in the next few hours, no one can point any fingers in your direction."

"Why should I care?"

"Because Sanders has an offer for you. A sweet offer, to compensate you for what you've given up this past year, and to make sure you come out of this on top. Regardless of what you may think of me right now, Dave, I've really grown to like you. And, as of tomorrow you're a real American hero. I don't want to see you do something stupid while you're still angry and confused that could wind up hurting you down the road."

"Then when can I get out of here?"

"In a few hours. I'll come for you personally, and then you can go home to Julia. And then, tomorrow hopefully, we can all sit down on a conference call with Sanders and figure out our next steps."

"I guess I don't have much choice, do I? See you in a few hours, then."

"Tomorrow will be a much brighter day, Dave. For all of us."

82

The war was taking longer than Marc had thought. The number of players online plummeted after the first hour or so, but there were still several thousand players finishing up their missions, particularly across China. The swan goose drones had been scattered throughout the country, and as daybreak arrived over China they started launching attacks on airfields, shipyards and a wide variety of other military assets. China's limited nuclear strike capabilities were among the first to be targeted, quickly taking out the country's ability to deliver a strategic response to the U.S. assault.

As a result of the delays, Sanders refused to release Dave until well after three the next morning. Marc decided to have him brought down to join them in the makeshift war room Carla had put together in the kitchen. The outside exits were sealed, and Dave didn't have access to any kind of communications equipment, so any danger to the secrecy of the project was minimal.

The war room was made up largely of flat screen displays scavenged from other offices, plus a couple of televisions tuned to the major news stations. So far there had been little in the way of news reports about the extensive military action that had broken out that evening from the Middle East all the way to North Korea. If you were counting on CNN to tell you what was happening in the world, you would have thought the entire planet was peaceful and calm that night.

One of the computer screens showed a graphic outline of Asia and territories immediately adjacent. Red dots highlighted current areas of action, while grey dots indicated places that had already been hit. It seemed like most of Russia and China had been bathed in grey. Another monitor showed the number of players still active in various locations. As the red dots turned gray across the map, the number of players slowly diminished.

Dave was still full of questions. "So how is this not Russia and China's Pearl Harbor? Their day of infamy? It all just seems like one big sneak attack to me."

Marc had already been through that with Sanders when he was finally read into the last details of the war a few weeks before. "I think that all depends upon your definition of sneak attack. Certainly, we didn't give them any warning that we were coming. But when in war do you call up your enemy and say 'Hey, be keeping an eye out for us at this place and this time?' By that standard, D-Day was a sneak attack."

Dave was undeterred. "Yeah, but by D-Day we were at war. That isn't the case here."

"You're right, Dave. But the fact is, the United States has been conducting military operations against our enemies non-stop since World War II, and none of them have been declared wars. Think of Vietnam, for example. So that's not the important issue, here. Look, I'm not going to argue about this, mainly because I'm not equipped to say whether this was right or wrong. That's for people much smarter than me. But I do know that the official message is that the U.S. is simply responding to a long series of unilateral provocations on the part of our enemies. The Ukraine is a perfect example of this — Russia just seized Crimea from Ukrainian control right out from under our noses, and then dared us to do anything about it. Well, tonight they got their payback." He walked up to the map and tapped several red dots lighting up in southern Crimea. "Those are A10 Warthog-type drone strikes in support of the Ukrainian army, taking out opposition tanks and anti-personnel carriers."

"We have A10 drones?" Dave asked incredulously.

"Well, not exactly," Marc answered. "Smaller aircraft, with far less firepower, camouflaged to fool the naked eye into thinking they're just flocks of birds. But, you know, it only takes one Hellfire missile to ruin a tank commander's entire day. And the Crimean sky is literally swarming with them right now, like a plague of locusts."

Dave carefully considered all that he had just learned. "But what I don't get is, why go to all the bother of conning me into writing the Xbox code? Why didn't your group just do it in-house?"

"You don't think we tried? Carla's been pounding away on that for three years. In fact, up until she moved out to Austin to coordinate with you on the back end, her team was still trying to hack together some kind of front end interface. And failing. It was all happening well before I came on board with this project, but my understanding is that Carla herself came up with the idea for the game company, to see if it might work out better to bring fresh young minds to bear on the problem. And still, of the four

294

programmers that we recruited to try out her idea, you were the only one that succeeded."

"But why Xbox? And why make it into a game? Why not just use the drone pilots the military already has on staff?"

"Dave, the military is currently training substantially more drone pilots every year than real pilots, but that is still a very small number. They even gave up years ago on requiring all drone pilots to be officers. The manpower simply wasn't there. And that was just for normal drone operations. To make *this* work, to attack worldwide, simultaneously, every major weapons system our enemies had in place, we needed *big* numbers. And the gamers gave us those numbers. By the way, we did use our drone pilots, and our existing drone control software, for the most critical missions. Missions that required a higher degree of delicacy, or targets we couldn't afford to miss. And that added up to only a small percentage of the total missions we flew tonight."

Dave thought about that. "All those players, that adds up to a humongous number of drones. Where did they all come from?"

Marc laughed. "I'm glad you asked that, Dave. Here's the really funny part. Almost all of the drones were built in China. We created several fake toy companies that contracted with Chinese factories to build them, at least the smaller drones. But, of course, we kept the control board and munitions manufacturing here at home. Couldn't let the Chinese get their hands on *those* designs!"

"So the Chinese built the very weapons we used to attack them?" Dave asked.

"Yeah, but that's not the really funny part. You know all about sovereign debt, right, the idea that the U.S. government can't afford to default on its debts to other nations?"

Dave indicated that he did.

"Okay, so over the past decade or so China has been buying up American assets and underwriting our exploding national debt. That's been a real problem for Washington, because if interest rates went back up, we could find ourselves upside down in a hurry, shoveling out more in interest payments than we collect in taxes. And defaulting on our debt wasn't an option, unless we wanted to totally wipe out our economy for a generation or so. Turn the United States into a Greece."

"So doesn't this war make that a real problem for us?" Dave wondered.

"Quite the opposite. You see, there is one exception to the debt default problem. If a nation declares war on us, we get to repudiate all of our debts to them, plus seize all of their assets in the United States—"

Dave looked up with keen interest. "And China—"

"Just fifteen minutes ago, China officially declared war. We suckered them into it."

"So we not only wiped them out militarily, we crushed them economically as well."

"Yeah, and here's the truly funny part. The drones they built for us — we gave them a ten percent deposit on the orders, but we still haven't paid them the balance. So, for all intents and purposes, the Chinese not only *built* the weapons we used to destroy them, they *paid* for them, too."

83

By the time Dave was allowed to head back home, Marc felt too tired to monitor the tail end of the action, so he headed home himself. Elle was still asleep, so he decided to grab a few hours of shut-eye himself before confronting her with the truth. Dave already knew about Marc's year of non-stop deceptions, which meant Julia would know about it very soon, as well. And that, in turn, meant that Elle would not be far behind. Better she hear it from him than from somebody else. At least he could control how the message was delivered.

Marc was out of bed and sipping on a cup of hot coffee when Elle finally woke up and joined him in the living room. *Now or never,* he decided. But he was barely into the middle of his quick explanation when the fiery redhead in Elle exploded.

"You bastard! You lying bastard!" Elle picked up a paperweight and flung it at Marc's head, just missing as he ducked out of the way.

"Elle, just give me a moment to explain—" He dodged another missile.

"I don't want to hear any more of your *lies!* Just *get out*!"

"Elle, I—"

"*Leave!* I never want to see you again, Marc Cullen! If that even *is* your real name!"

"Of course it's my real name. Elle, it was just a job I had to do—"

Another object came flying across the room at him, and Marc decided it might be a good idea to beat a hasty retreat for the time being. Give her some time to absorb it all, to blow off some steam, then try again later. Something heavy crashed into the door just a moment after he closed it behind him.

84

Later in the day, as Marc was just drumming up the courage to give Elle a call, he got a reply email from her on his phone, a response to an earlier email he had sent her, explaining everything that had happened.

"Marc," she began. "I've been thinking this through, trying to work through everything you told me, and I just don't think this will work out. I know you said it was all about your job, about having to lie to keep the project secret, but I just can't go forward any longer with someone I can't trust. Not knowing from moment to moment whether you're being honest with me. And not just with me. You put Dave in a very dangerous position, forced him to take some very serious risks. Both personal and financial. I just don't think that's the kind of person I can commit my life to. You aren't the person I thought I was in love with.

"I've already moved my stuff out. I'll be staying with friends until I can move back to California. I'll try to get accepted into the Cal Berkeley MBA program, maybe. Or just get another job for now.

"You can have the furniture and all the rest of the stuff in the apartment. I don't even want to deal with any of that anymore, have anything at all to do with it. It would only remind me of what I thought we had together. Of what I lost. Of what we both lost.

"Goodbye, Marc"

Boy, I guess I was dead wrong about this, he thought. *I don't think there's any way I can fix this. And I just let the very best thing that ever happened to me slip right through my hands.*

85

The next morning, Dave had finally recovered somewhat from all the drama and surprises, so Julia talked him into breakfast at Kerbey Lane Cafe, just off 37th Street.

"So, Dave, what are you going to do?" Julia had been very concerned when he didn't answer her phone calls two nights earlier. She was even more concerned for him when he got home and told her about everything that had happened. He had just seemed so vulnerable, so *lost*. And the worst part was, she wasn't sure how to help him.

"I don't know, Jules." Dave glanced down at his coffee, then reached across the table and took her left hand in his. "I had a long talk with Sanders yesterday, and he offered me a bonus for the work I did on the software. A bonus that, quite frankly, dwarfs the money I got out of Google. He also suggested that the Defense Intelligence Agency or some other department might want to contract with Rocketship to do what we originally planned, modify the code to create a war games simulator."

"Is that something you want to do?" She reached over and layered his hand between hers.

"It might be. I don't know. It's all too soon. I told him I would look it over and get back to him in a few weeks. He seemed okay with that."

"What about Marc? What's going to happen with him?"

"Well, for starters, he's out at Rocketship. We signed all the papers late yesterday. Regardless of what happens going forward, he and I are done."

"So what's going on with Marc and Elle?"

Dave gave her a small shrug. "You may know more about that than I do. From what he told me, she took it pretty hard. Worse than I did, even. She's evidently moved out and is heading back to California."

"I'm not surprised. I can't imagine how badly she was hurt. I had the impression she was planning on getting married just as soon as you guys finished the launch. When we were up in Dallas, she was even talking about babies. I still can't believe he lied to her like that. Lied to all of us!"

"Well, Jules, putting all of Marc's lies aside, after all that we just went through, the important thing is... I still have you in my life. Maybe it's time *we* started talking about marriage and babies." He gave her a warm and suggestive smile.

"Hmmmmm," she purred. "Marriage we can discuss, but if you think for a moment I'm going to ruin *this* gorgeous figure just to pop out babies for you, then, I'm warning you, you better pony up for a huge ring, buster!"

"Guess I better lock down that day job with Sanders, after all," Dave laughed.

86

Last night had been some long-overdue R&R, Sanders thought, as he watched her crawl out of bed and pad quietly toward the bathroom. The warm morning light coming from the window glowed easily through her translucent ivory peignoir, revealing the soft and luscious curves underneath.

"Hey, honey, why get going so soon? It's been so long. Why don't we just — sleep in a little longer?" The only response he heard was the sound of the shower turning on. "You know, you can always reset that meeting for later today..."

Sanders gave up and wandered into the bathroom himself. She had just dropped her nightgown to the floor and was testing the temperature of the shower. He stepped up behind her, wrapping his arms around her chest and waist. Part of him pressed suggestively between her firm buttocks and started to stir once again. He lifted her red locks and nuzzled the nape of her neck, reaching up playfully to nibble on her ear.

"Actually, Elle, a shower seems like a pretty good idea..."

acknowledgments

The idea for this book has been banging around in my head for over four decades, but I could never seem to find the time, energy or talent to finally get it down on paper. At least, now I have the time and energy...

As always, the little talent for the written word I do have would have been a complete embarrassment but for the love and attention this book received from my amazing editor, Kara Vaught. Without her, the English language would lie mangled and bloody at my metaphorical feet.

As always, my everlasting thanks to Elizabeth, my greatest cheerleader, my inspiration, my best friend forever, and the keeper of my heart.

about the author

Rene Fomby started his career as a pioneer in video gaming and personal computers. A member of the team that designed the computer that ultimately became the Apple Macintosh, he also served as the Director of the National Healthcare Database under the auspices of the Department of Health and Human Services, and his software company was a strategic partner with Microsoft and Hewlett Packard in the field of healthcare computing. Currently, Rene practices criminal defense and civil litigation across the state of Texas. An accomplished member of the State Bar's Probono College, he takes on the nail biting cases other lawyers turn away. More importantly, Rene is a winemaker, sailor, private pilot, helicopter dad and loving husband, and is currently owned by two dogs and one very feisty Maine Coon cat.

other books by rene fomby

Resumed Innocent

private eyes

coming soon

Reflecting the Dead

Revelations, Revolutions